RAIDER WORKED THE LEVER
OF THE WINCHESTER
UNTIL IT WAS EMPTY.

Schaeffer was dead. Curley clutched a shattered shoulder.

"Pick up your rifle, Curley."

The panicked clerk couldn't move. Raider drew his Remington as the driverless wagon shot out of the gap, swaying wildly. A lucky shot carried away Raider's Stetson. He emptied the pistol as the horses screamed in terror and the wagon began to keel over.

Raider clung to the seat for dear life as four tons of dead weight crashed down the side of the mountain.

J.D. HARDIN

SILVER TOMBSTONES

PLAYBOY
PAPERBACKS

Published simultaneously in the United States and Canada by Playboy Paperbacks, New York, New York. Printed in the United States of America. Library of Congress Catalog Card Number: 81-80672. First edition.

Books are available at quantity discounts for promotional and industrial use. For further information, write to Premium Sales, Playboy Paperbacks, 1633 Broadway, New York, New York 10019.

ISBN: 0-872-16839-5

First printing August 1981.

CHAPTER ONE

Half a day down from Coffin Canyon, carved from the living rock by coolie labor and Number Four Coarse Grain black powder, the narrow road clung to the face of the mountain. The sun beat down on the Sierras and seared the eight heavily armed men who guarded the silver wagon.

"Damned hellish, O'Toole, fer fust June," growled Burt McAfee, the wagon's wizened, whiskery driver. He spat a stream of tobacco juice over the side of the road and shaded his eyes to fix the sun in the glare-filled sky.

"Been drivin' wagon an' skinnin' mules in these hills an' down in the Mother Lode thutty years," said Burt. "Ain't never seen it so blesset hot this early."

Raider grunted as Burt addressed him by the name he was using: John O'Toole. The Pinkerton agent rode the wagon's box, while two mounted riders led them by a hundred yards, and another pair trailed close enough to be in danger from loose pebbles kicked up by the heavy iron tires. Six horses leaned into the traces to pull 8,000 pounds—a ton and a half of wagon and riders and 80,000 ounces of silver ingots—up a slight rise. The face of the mountain was close enough for Raider to reach out and pluck grass from a crevice, while the outside wheels, forty-four inches in front and fifty-two inches in the rear, were only a couple of feet from the edge of the precipice.

His stomach sour and his mood black, Raider silently cursed Doc Weatherbee for handing him the shitty end of the stick once again. It had been his

Pinkerton partner's idea to check in with the Denver office, when Raider had wanted to drop out of sight for a while. The partners had just wrapped up a goddamn difficult case, and they sure as hell had the time coming. But somehow Doc, the sonofabitch, had learned that William Pinkerton was in town, so the silly bastard had had to go looking for a pat on the back.

Which he hadn't gotten. Raider and Doc, Doc's apothecary wagon and Judith, his mule, had been on the next train west before Raider had managed to check out his room at the Brown Palace Hotel or renew acquaintances with Mattie Silks, Denver's most famous and popular madam. Raider had heard that Mattie had taken to wearing a diamond-encrusted cross around her neck; a gaudy and garish symbol for a woman engaged in the oldest profession, but supposedly a sight to see.

Damn Doc's hide to hell and back!

The wagon lurched over a rock, bouncing Raider and Burt against each other and drawing a stifled moan from Ed Curley, in the bed. Dutch Schaeffer, the other guard riding the wagon, laughed as paunchy, middle-aged Curley, recruited from the pay office of the Coffin Queen silver mine, rearranged his pile of gunnysacks to cushion the misery of bleeding piles.

"Why the hell didn't you bring a featherbed for your asshole, Curley?"

Curley ignored the young hardcase as he settled himself gingerly atop the layers of silver ingots that were covered by a canvas tarp. Raider ignored both of them. He straightened the fancy Ithaca shotgun across his lap and picked up the Winchester that had toppled across his Middleton boots. His favorite Remington .44 was in its holster.

Burt spat, the brown liquid arcing into space fell a hundred feet down the sheer face of the mountain before it splattered against a jagged boulder. Five hundred feet below, a stream sparkled bright with the last of the spring runoff. The snow capping the peaks of the surrounding mountains would stay there until dooms-day.

Raider eyeballed the sun: coming up on noon. At this very moment Doc was no doubt sitting on his ass in Virginia City's finest hotel, filling his gut with prime steak, while his partner could look forward to cold beef on day-old bread and warm beer. He swallowed a belch.

In the best of times, Raider wasn't too fond of Doc, although for four years they had been together through places thick and thin. Riding a goddamn silver ship-ment down the spine of a mountain with roughnecks and hardcases and a stinking old man had to count as one of the thinner. More than once, the partners had been known to mix it up, and one of Raider's teeth was still loose from the last time Doc poked him in the jaw. He tested it, happy that the pain was almost gone.

Burt shot a sideways look at the tall, rangy man be-side him as Raider tilted his black Stetson forward to shield his piercing black eyes while he scanned the road below. He had doffed his jacket, but the heat of the day made his shirt stick to his body. Raider brushed away a fly intent on investigating his black moustache, despite a wealth of more interesting odors that rose from Burt's unwashed clothes.

Behind him, Ed Curley dried his hands on his trou-sers and picked up his shotgun, a battered single-shot 20-gauge someone had scrounged from a saloon. Ed wondered if the others knew he had never fired a gun in his life. Dutch Schaeffer, no more than twenty years old, slid down on the base of his spine and pulled his hat low over his eyes, while Burt muttered to himself, spraying tobacco juice.

"Man orta be sociable." Burt's Adam's apple bounced as he chomped at his words with toothless gums. Then he cackled and slapped the old Colt Dra-goon that banged his knee.

"B'God, boys, I hope those bastards do try us!"

It was perhaps the twentieth time Burt had made the statement since the wagon had left the yard of the Coffin Queen at first light that morning. This was not the main road down to Carson City, but one that would take them twenty miles and an extra day out of their way. In the past ten weeks, four of the Coffin Queen's shipments of silver to the Carson City mint had been ambushed, the drivers and escorts wiped out. Three of the wagons had been found smashed in canyon bottoms. There was still no trace of the fourth.

Three weeks ago Junius Coffin himself had made a trip to Denver to secure the aid of the Pinkertons; this was why Raider, pretending to be drifter John O'Toole, rode shotgun on this goddamn wagon, while Doc, sniffing out gossip that might yield a clue to the man or men behind the Coffin Queen's troubles, took his pampered ease in Virginia City, two mountains over.

None of the other mines of the district had suffered similar losses, which made it certain somebody had it in for the Coffin family. The Queen had been discovered by C. C. Coffin twenty years before, a year after the more famous Comstock Lode was found. In those twenty years, the Queen had produced almost as much by itself as had all of the mines of the more famous Lode, but Comstock was there first and had grabbed off the glory.

Junius Coffin and his younger brothers, Jasper and Jonathan, had taken control of the mine ten years ago, although their father was still alive and still lived in the big house that overlooked the Number One shaft and its growing mountain of tailings. It pained Junius to talk about his father, who was rumored to be as crazy as a hoot owl—and positively agonized him to know that C. C. had remarried last year after six short months of widowerhood. He never talked about his stepmother.

Only Junius and Raider had known that the shipment would leave this morning—Junius swore that not even his brothers had been told. And Raider had roused the guards from their beds an hour before daybreak, herding them through breakfast so they'd have no chance to spill what they knew. Unless someone had got hold of the coded telegram Raider had left with Junius to be sent to Doc, there was no way anyone else could know this was the day. Yet a worrisome itch crawled along Raider's spine. He could smell trouble in the air.

They were ready for it: the wagon was a rolling arsenal. They lacked only a Gatling gun, and that only because Junius Coffin had been unable to bring pressure to bear on the nearest army post in time. Two boxes of shells for the shotgun and the Winchester were between Raider's feet, and his gun belt was full as well.

The situation called for undercover work, of course; only the Coffin brothers knew the Pinkertons had been brought in on the job.

Dutch Schaeffer stirred and brought a railroad watch from his vest pocket; then he dug into a gunnysack and passed out sandwiches and beer. Raider chomped savagely on the stale bread, ignoring the twinge in his tooth. The butter was on the point of turning, and the food did neither his mood nor his stomach any good. He worked the wire from a rubber stopper and drained a bottle of hot beer, belched mightily, and stood to throw the empty into the canyon, venting his anger. The bottle arced high, turning over and over and glinting in the sun; but the crash was drowned by the rumbling of the tires.

Another hour passed slowly as the wagon rolled down the back side of the mountain. Ed Curley managed to doze, and even Burt was silent for a time, until the road made a wide sweep around a bulge in the mountainside.

"Graveyard Gap comin' up."

Burt loosened the Dragoon in its holster and checked to make sure the extra cylinder, already primed with ball and percussion caps, was ready to snap into place. One of the outriders carried a pair of Navy Colts, model of 1851, but they had been converted from cap-and-ball to the modern brass cartridges. Only Burt, of this crew, clung to the old-fashioned system. The ancient revolver, scarred from the Mexican and Civil wars and weighing four pounds and one ounce, was almost more than he could manage.

Raider tensed as the wagon came down the Gap, a slash that cut deep into the face of the mountain. It had been given its name because it had been the burying place for the Chinamen who died while building the road. The Gap was an ancient wound almost a mile wide and a thousand yards deep that had been filled in by erosion and landslide, and now there was a heavy stand of spruce and lodgepole pine that came down within fifty yards of the road. A small stream cut through a meadow, crossing the road and turning to mist as it fell over the face of the mountain.

The trees were thick enough to hide a small army. The hackles bristled across Raider's neck, and he muttered a warning to the others. The horsemen fell back, gathering around the wagon.

"Don't like it," said Burt soberly, eying the woods.

Raider grunted and cocked the Ithaca—a fancily engraved bird gun that had been forced on him by Junius Coffin. He had seen the likes of it in a catalogue at fifteen hundred dollars, but gold and silver inlay wouldn't help it shoot one bit better.

"Whip up the team," he said quietly.

Burt snapped the reins. "Heyup, Lucifer! Le's go!"

For several minutes, nothing happened; yet, as the wagon splashed through the stream, Raider was sure all hell was about to break loose. A sudden breeze swept through the Gap, giving a brief respite from the heat. Two hundred yards and they'd be out. Raider's chest ached, as though a rifle were trained on his heart—

"*Aiyayayayaya!*"

A band of Indians broke from the forest with a war whoop and the shattering bark of repeating rifles that cut down two of the escort while the other men stared in shock.

"Apaches!" yelled Burt, struggling to pull his Dragoon from his holster.

"Apaches, hell!" said Raider, dropping behind the seat as Burt let off a single shot that went ten feet over the tops of the trees. "Since when do Apaches shoe their goddamn horses?"

He raised the Ithaca, while Schaeffer stood and emptied his shotgun much too early and to no effect. The attackers rode down on the wagon, four swerving to outrun the pounding team and cut off their escape from the Gap.

"Hee*yaw*, Lucifer!" yelled Burt. "Come on, dammit! *Hee*yawwwwp—"

The old man's yell turned to a strangled cry, and he toppled forward, falling off the box and bouncing from the hindquarters of the rear horses, landing on the shafts. There was a thud as Burt bounced again and hit the front of the wagon; then he dropped, the wagon lurching as it rolled over his frail body, spoiling Schaeffer's aim as he fired his Winchester.

Raider could see the sweat making runnels in the war paint of the phony Indians. All of the escort were down. He counted to three as the nearest attacker rode closer; then he stood and let loose with both barrels of the Ithaca. A look of astonishment crossed the attacker's face as his guts were blasted into ground meat, and then he fell from his horse, forcing two of his fellows to swerve wide and their shots to miss target.

The driverless wagon headed down the last stretch of Graveyard Gap as Raider dropped the Ithaca and steadied the Winchester against the back of the seat.

Schaeffer was dead, his face blasted away. Curley clutched a shattered shoulder, moaning piteously.

"Pick up your rifle, Curley!"

The panicked clerk couldn't move. Raider worked the lever of the Winchester until it was empty, and two more of the attackers fell. He drew the Remington as the wagon shot out of the Gap, out of control and swaying wildly. It was impossible to sight on a target as the runaway horses plunged down the suddenly steeper grade—and then a lucky shot carried away Raider's Stetson.

He cursed as the hammer of the Remington fell on a discharged cartridge and grabbed the Winchester again, levering shells into it as one of the attackers leaped over the back of the wagon, foolishly daring death—

The man was carried back by Raider's shot, dead when his skull cracked open on a rock in the road. The road curved; the wagon wheels smashed a small rock and began to rise into the air as the horses screamed in terror.

Raider clung to the seat, unable to use the rifle as the wagon rose to the point of no return. Then one of the rear horses went down, tangled in the shafts. Four tons of dead weight heeled over and began to roll down the mountain . . .

CHAPTER TWO

"Mornin', Dr. Weatherbee. Telegram come in fer ya."

Doc Weatherbee paused, swaying, on the bottom step of the Virginia House's ornately carved mahogany grand staircase, clinging to the statue on the newel-post, squinting his eyes against the agony of a champagne headache, and peering in the direction of the desk clerk who had just addressed him.

"Come in 'bout eight o'clock," the clerk added. "Figgered you didn't want t' be bothered with business matters this mornin'."

The clerk's smirk irritated Doc. He turned his head to look at the statue, a plaster replica of Hiram Power's *California*—and realized that his hand cupped the naked innocent's backside.

Doc snatched his hand away, embarrassed, and advanced to the desk, drawing out his watch. He popped the cover: almost noon. The telegram had arrived four hours before.

"Thank you," he said dryly, surprised at the sourness of his mood. "Hereafter, please send any messages as soon as they arrive."

Rebuked, the clerk held to the corner of the envelope a moment longer than necessary. He peered nearsightedly through pince-nez that were fastened to his alpaca jacket by a black silk ribbon, as though no longer certain of his first identification of the hotel's most flamboyant guest. Doc tugged, the wire was released, and he turned away, seething, to run a finger beneath the flap. He continued his stroll toward the hotel dining room as he scanned the coded message from Raider.

13

Only Raider and Junius Coffin, and of course the Denver and Chicago offices, knew that Doc was in Virginia City, masquerading as the agent for a European mining syndicate. He was uncomfortable in the unfamiliar role, but the decision had been made by Denver that he should abandon his usual cover, the apothecary wagon and Judith, his mule. An itinerant peddler of homeopathic remedies and electric invigorators would scarcely be welcome in the parlors of Virginia City's mine operators.

The Studebaker wagon and Judith were now in a livery in the town of Washoe, several miles away, the colorful advertising signs covered. Doc missed Judith. He had been in Virginia City three weeks, the longest mule and owner had ever been separated.

The message was short. It wasn't necessary for Doc to return to his room to refer to his code book, usually hidden, along with his own telegraph equipment and his camera and developing supplies, in the special compartment in the bottom of the wagon.

Unaware that he was being watched by a dozen pairs of idle eyes, Doc entered the dining room. Today he was impeccably dressed in a tricot summer suit of powder blue with white piping, a silk shirt with blue pinstripes, a blue silk paisley vest, a flawlessly tied cravat—retied four times this morning before Doc had been satisfied that it was passable—with its genuine if small diamond stickpin, and his favorite pearl gray curled-brim derby. His boots were freshly blacked, his hair slicked down with Brilliantine. He had carefully shaved, nicking only his Adam's apple. Only his red eyes and the way he winced when dishes clattered revealed his hangover.

The Virginia House was as opulent as Doc was flashy, with marble mantels and red velvet hangings, a crystal chandelier from Paris that put to shame the one in the San Francisco Opera House, and solid silver spittoons, placed there for the convenience of the mining gentry. Ensconced in the Comstock Suite was a leading prima donna from a French opera company, here to give the hinterlands a week of grand opera. Doc had caught the performance the night before and then had been invited to a recital and a post-performance midnight supper on Millionaire's Row. The French champagne served with the supper was responsible for his hangover, although it had left nothing to be desired. Unfortunately, he could not say the same for the guest of honor's musical range.

Virginia City was no stranger to grand opera. Most of the famous entertainers stopped off here for at least a few days during their western tours. Most recently, the silver kings had applauded the divine Miss Sarah Bernhardt, while posters in the saloons advertised comic Eddie Foy's appearance the next week at the music hall.

Virginia City was still the queen of the silver boom towns, a raw, wide-open frontier town in many ways. Its population had peaked at 30,000 before the disastrous fire of 1875. The census was now down by a third, although more than thirty-six millions in silver had been shipped out of the Comstock Lode in each of the last two years.

In its short twenty years of life, Virginia City had gone from boom to bust to boom again. The town's boosters spoke with pride of the nearly four hundred millions in silver that had been shipped out of the Lode, with admiration of Adolph Sutro's four-mile tunnel— completed last year after nineteen years of digging to drain the lowest levels of the mines—and with astonishment of the two great pipelines, one seven miles long and the other thirty-one and a half miles long, which brought the necessary water from the High Sierras to Mount Davidson. The pipelines made the mines possible, for the mountain had been honeycombed by shafts.

The boosters also spoke of the city's six churches

and its up-to-date schools. The cruder bragged about the one hundred saloons that catered to the miners and the occasional rancher and his cowhands. Even Doc was impressed by the contrast of wild, raucous saloons and branches of San Francisco's finest department stores, of shops featuring the latest Paris fashions for the miners' ladies, and gambling joints. Any first-time visitor was sure to be shown the Territorial Enterprise, where ten years before, Mark Twain had been one of the reporters; and the locals pointed out the steep streets and the long wooden staircases built to carry pedestrians from one block to the next.

The hotel dining room was half-full. Doc was shown to a small table almost hidden in the fronds of a rubber plant. He nodded at several acquaintances but refused two invitations to join a party. After the night before, he was in no mood to listen to small talk.

Despite his queasy stomach, he gave his order for steak and eggs; then he reread Raider's wire while the waiter poured coffee from a silver pot and filled his crystal tumbler with ice water. Doc expected just two messages from his Pinkerton partner: word that a silver shipment was on its way, or a call for help. The latter would mean Raider had managed to crack the ring that was ambushing the Coffin Queen's shipments.

The silver was on its way to the mint at Carson City. Doc sighed, folding the yellow message form and stowing it in an inner pocket. He had hoped Raider was having better luck in Coffin Canyon than he was having in Virginia City.

In the three weeks since Doc had climbed down from the parlor car of the Virginia & Truckee, the richest short line railroad in the United States, he had learned that the Coffins, father and sons, had few friends in the Comstock. But Virginia City's mine owners expressed shock at the raids on the Coffin Queen's shipments.

"CeeCee Coffin is and was a lyin', shirt-stealin' bas-tard!" declared Judge Cletis Roundtree, principal partner in the Lady Gay. "He'd rob the pennies out of a poor box and tell the minister a church that couldn't protect its money didn't deserve donations."

"He'd sell chalked water to orphans for milk and charge them deposit on the rusty can," had been the succinct opinion of another of the pioneers.

"Hell," said a third, "CeeCee'd give a blind man a twenty-cent piece and take change for a quarter dollar."

"Still," offered Doc, pressing the judge's boil to see if he could force an eruption, "Cyrus Coffin is supposed to be a shrewd operator."

"CccCee ain't got the sense God give a half-witted billy goat," said the judge. "He's just the luckiest son-ofabitch ever to trip over his own feet and fall into a glory hole."

"Do you know him personally?" Doc asked.

"To my perpetual misfortune, sir. We come around the Horn together in forty-nine—Argonauts, they called us then."

"Hell," said the second man, "CeeCee run out on a wife and seven kids, left 'em flat in Boston. Left her to raise the brood by herself, without a penny of help, for ten years, till he struck it rich at the canyon."

"The boys run the operation now," said the judge. "Junius—he's the oldest—is a sly one. He forced Cee-Cee to sign over the mine in—when was it, Homer? —seventy-one?"

"Yep, seventy-one," said Homer, who would not have contradicted the judge if it had been 1861. "They say, though, that CeeCee's gone crazy."

"Not too crazy to marry hisself a chippie," someone else had said. "German woman, ain't she, Judge? Von Deff, or somethin' like that."

"Von Dorf," the judge had said, chomping on a cigar. "She's American—married two, three times 'fore she latched onto CeeCee. Don't know much about her, 'cept she come into the canyon 'bout a year back, just after the Queen went back into full operation."

"Fine figger of a woman, I'm told," the third man had said, chuckling. "Must've upset her some to learn CeeCee signed ever'thing over to the boys."

Listening, Doc had decided the judge knew a great deal more than he pretended. Cletis Roundtree seemed well informed on the operations and the kitchen gossip of every mine operator in the district. This was why Doc had carefully arranged a barber shop meeting, and why he had spent most of these three weeks cultivating the judge's friendship.

But in three weeks, Doc had done no more than compile a long list of men who publicly admitted their dislike of the Coffins. No closer to learning something useful than he had been at the first meeting with Junius Coffin, in Denver. At the moment Doc envied Raider. At least his partner was doing something useful. Not for the first time, he considered giving up here and joining Raider in Carson City to plan a new course of action.

"CeeCee's boys had some bad years," the judge had declared on another occasion. "Congress passin' the Bland-Allison Act last year saved their hides."

It was unnecessary to elaborate; everyone in the West knew that the Bland-Allison Act had saved the generally depressed silver industry. Only Virginia City had not suffered the depression of the last few years.

The act authorized the purchase of two to four million dollars' worth of silver bullion a month, to be used only for coining into silver dollars. It was the first time since 1873 that a dollar had been coined, and eastern interests protested the act as a sop to the mining interests. They were right, for the silver dollar had been discontinued as an unnecessary coin, along with the two-cent piece, the three-cent silver trime, and the silver half dime. And after little more than a year, the bags of new dollars were piling up in the vaults of the Treasury Department, for only the West preferred the heavy ring of hard money to the rustle of bank notes. Levi Strauss had been forced to put canvas pockets into his jeans because gold and silver coins wore out cotton too fast.

Breakfast arrived. Doc dug in with vigor, giving no thought to the trail rations Raider was even now sharing. The food eased his stomach, and as he ate, he mentally composed the journal entry he would make to bring the case record up to date. Until now, the reports to Wagner in Chicago had been short, one code word that meant "no developments."

Inner man satisfied, Doc signaled the waiter for more coffee and spent a moment of idle chatter with an acquaintance departing from the dining room. He drew out a cigar case and from that took an Old Virginia cheroot, sniffing the strong tobacco appreciatively before he wet the end and fumbled a lucifer from his pocket. The waiter hurried over to light the cigar as though afraid Doc would strike the match on the gleaming varnish of the wainscoting.

"Dr. Weatherbee?"

Doc looked up to see a buxom but handsome woman in her forties standing over him. She wore a watered-silk dress of dark blue that was too fancy for this time of day, and her dark auburn hair was piled on top of her head. Her generous bosom supported a triple strand of pearls, and stones of half a dozen hues glittered on her fingers.

Her voice was a rich contralto. "I heard the waiter address you by name. You are a medical doctor, aren't you?"

Astonished, Doc scrambled to his feet and found that his six feet brought his eyes only an inch above hers. The dress seemed garish, but her manner was cultured. And the jewels were real.

"It's my daughter, Zelzah," she continued, batting her eyes at him shamelessly. "She seems to have come down with something, doctor. I would be most appreciative if you could spare a moment to look in on her."

"Uh . . . I'm not a practicing physician, madam," said Doc, floundering. "And I am a follower of Hahnemann—the founder of homeopathy. But I'm afraid you have the better of me, Miss . . . ?"

"Coffin," she said, uttering the name with some surprise, as though he should know it. Which of course, he did. "*Mrs.* Cyrus C. C. Coffin, Doctor."

"I do not have my medical kit with me. I understand the hotel has a physician on call," said Doc, nonplussed.

"But I am a believer in homeopathy!" said Helena von Dorf Coffin exuberantly. "Please, Dr. Weatherbee, just a moment of your time, I beg you."

Doc shrugged in embarrassed surrender. He dropped his scarcely tasted cheroot in the nearest silver spittoon and followed CeeCee Coffin's wife from the dining room, telling himself that this meeting had to be a coincidence.

CHAPTER THREE

The shaft of the wagon snapped and broke free of the traces as the rear wheel slipped over the edge of the road. The horses scrambled free as the massive load began to roll in slow motion, a majestic sight to anyone who might have been watching from below. During the roll, the canvas cover clung to the silver while Ed Curley and Dutch Schaeffer were thrown clear.

The wagon hit them again on the second roll, and the silver ingots shifted. They began to spill as the wagon continued to turn over, end over end now, leaving a silver-bright trail of treasure that stretched halfway down the side of the mountain.

Raider was scarcely aware of the fate of the treasure as he jumped clear, tucking his chin down and wrapping his arms about his knees. He hit on his heels in the loose shale and somersaulted three times before he hit hard and bounced into the air again. The sky and the mountain wheeled dizzily before his eyes, and the Remington flew from his holster when he hit again, in a clump of manzanita that clung to a narrow ledge fifteen feet down the sheer face of the mountain. Below, two hundred feet straight down, the bottom of the canyon was studded with broken boulders.

"Sonofabitch! I knew we shoulda' blocked the goddamn road!"

The raiding party reined up, and the leader cursed, watching the wagon disintegrate on its way to the bottom of the canyon, leaving a wheel here, the driver's box there, and a trail of silver ingots everywhere.

"Now what?" asked another of the false Indians. He

soothed his blowing horse, patting its neck. "That's a long goddamn climb."

"So get started!" said the leader. "We ain't got all day. Start earnin' your pay!"

"We already earned our pay," said a third, *sotto voce,* to a companion as he dismounted from his pony and took a lariat from the pommel. "How many of us got kilt?"

"Three," said the other, shrugging. "Nobody said gittin' rich was gonna be easy."

A clatter of iron-rimmed wheels sounded from the gap as the half-dozen surviving members of the raiding party brought ropes, snagged them around boulders, and then began the cautious climb down the mountain after the silver. A moment later, a stage appeared. The driver clambered down when it stopped, wasting a single look down the slope. Then he went to the tangled team of the silver wagon and began to unhitch the horses, slapping them on the rumps as he freed them.

"Hiyaaa! Git outa here!"

The horses broke into a run. By the time the driver returned to the stage, the first of the silver was coming up. He opened the doors, and reached in to break out the seats, then turned to accept the first ingot. He and the leader began to load the silver into the stage.

"Hey!"

The call came from one of those below who had scrabbled across the face of the mountain after two errant ingots and spotted Raider, lying face down in the manzanita.

"There's one of the bastards!"

"Is he alive?" called the leader.

"I dunno! He ain't movin'."

"Put a bullet in him to be sure."

The man was nearly fifty yards away, above the ledge. Not wanting to come any closer on the loose shale, he drew his pistol and sighted carefully. His gun bucked as he squeezed the trigger, and he saw Raider's body jump as the slug tore across his shoulder.

"That got the bastard!" he called. "If'n he ain't dead, he soon will be."

"All right, get to it—get the goddamn silver!"

In a daze, Raider heard the shouts of the men. A thousand brands burned into his body where he had struck on the rocks, where the sharp ends of manzanita dug into his flesh. Then he heard the gunshot and new fire burned across his shoulder blade. For a time he passed into blessed unconsciousness.

The sun moved, baking his flesh while he lay on the ledge. When he woke again, his lips were puffed and his tongue swollen. A manzanita stem was trying to drill straight through his belly. He lay still, listening to the grunting and the curses of the attackers as they labored to bring the last of the silver back up to the stage. After a time he dozed again, slipping into fevered dreams of hot baths and cold beer. In one, he slammed his fists again and again into Doc's bastardly face.

The last of the attackers pulled himself back onto the road. "That's it," he said. "I ain't goin' down no farther. Anybody wants the rest of that goddamn silver, they can go down and git it."

The stage rode low on its leather slings, threatening to bend the iron braces. The seats had been replaced, and the boot was filled, its canvas cover tied down. The six-horse team moved restlessly in the traces, snorting and blowing, as though aware of the load they would have to stop from running away on the trip down the mountain.

The leader stood on the edge of the road, shading his eyes to count the ingots scattered far below. He could see no more than twenty.

"Okay, let's get out of here," he said. "Get out of these phony Injun getups. We'll meet at Brannigan's ranch in three days for the payoff."

The men mounted and began to move off as the driver snapped his whip over the team. The stage creaked into motion, reluctantly. They took their dead with them. None spared another look at the mountain, or at the three bodies lying broken beneath a sky that harbored a dozen high dots as the carrion-eaters gathered for the feast.

Raider heard the stage driver's cursing and a last call or two from the horsemen as they rode off. An ant was investigating his face. It ran across his chin and started up his cheek toward his eye. He blinked violently, trying to scare it away, while he counted to a thousand, slowly. Only then did he try to move.

"Jesus Christ Almighty!"

Pain stabbed from a hundred places at once, and for a moment he thought he had broken a leg. But the knee was only wrenched; after a deep breath he gritted his teeth and managed to sit up.

Raider tested his wounded shoulder. The bullet had burned across the muscles, ripping through his shirt and coming out at the seam across the top. His fingers seemed numb as he worked them. He kept on opening and closing his fist, forcing his arm to obey, to respond. The pain didn't diminish, but his hand worked easier.

The manzanita was broken to form an almost perfect outline of his body. The ledge was no more than three feet wide and eight long. Raider looked over the ledge, straight down. There was no way down without a rope, unless he wanted to commit suicide. He hadn't quite reached that stage.

The only way out was up. But as he craned his neck, the fifteen feet up seemed as great as the two hundred feet down. He pulled himself painfully to his feet, swaying as a sharp pain stabbed through his kidneys. One hand against the face of the mountain, he relieved himself, and the pain diminished slightly. Then he swallowed and took stock of his situation.

He had lost his pistol, but he carried eight or ten

pounds of dead weight in his gun belt. He tested the cliff, which was dotted with brush that had established itself in the crevices. But when Raider grabbed the nearest branch and leaned his weight against it, the roots pulled out of the rotted rock. He tried again, reaching for a higher one—and cried out as pain exploded through every fiber of his body. He fell back onto the ledge.

Christ! Raider stared at the circling buzzards as they rode the air currents lower, now close enough to be seen in all their ugliness. None had landed yet, but it wouldn't be long. One circled out over the canyon, dropping until it was no more than twenty feet higher than Raider and a hundred feet away. At that distance, he could see its beady eyes glistening with hunger and with something else that might have been lust.

"Bastard!" he growled, fumbling a cartridge from his gun belt. He threw it, swallowing his breath as pain exploded again, and the cartridge bounced off the buzzard's breast feathers. The mighty pinions beat once, and the bird began the long climb back into the sky to wait a bit longer, unaffected by the dying creature's puny effort.

It was luck that the bullet had hit the buzzard, for Raider's cast had been wild and uncontrolled. He managed to sit up and lean against the face of the cliff. He must have dozed, for when he looked again, the sun had moved across the sky. His lips had cracked open under the heat. The buzzards were still there, in greater numbers than before—and then a rifle cracked once, and a dozen more birds took off from the slope with raucous cries.

"Go on!" cried a voice. "Git, y' wuthless hunks o' bone an' feathers, 'fore y' stink up th' mountain!"

"Hey!" Raider tried to call out, but only a rasping croak came from his throat. He went into a coughing spasm that sent new pain wracking through his chest.

Suddenly a rope came snaking down from the cliff,

nearly hitting him in the eye. He batted it away, and a moment later Burt McAfee peered over the ledge.

"Burt?" croaked Raider, amazed. But that was crazy. Burt was dead.

"You okay, mister?" asked a voice. Raider blinked several times and almost brought the grizzled face into focus; it still looked like Burt's, but the voice was different.

"I'm . . ." He swallowed several times, and the face withdrew. A moment later, a canteen came snaking down at the end of a rawhide tether.

"Take a drink," said the old man, reappearing.

Raider hastily unscrewed the cap and tilted the canteen to his lips, letting the refreshingly cold water spill over as he filled his mouth. The canteen had been filled recently from a mountain stream, probably within the half hour. The water burned like ice as it hit his belly. He wiped his mouth with the back of his hand, sighing.

"Thanks, mister," he said.

"You better be able to haul yerself outa there," said the old man, " 'cause I sure as hell ain't got the strength. Give it a try."

The canteen went dancing back up as Raider forced himself onto his feet. He swayed, but he managed to grab the rope in both hands, tugging. It was secured.

The old man watched, hands on knees, as Raider wrapped the rope about one arm and planted a foot against the cliff face. He closed his eyes for a moment and took several deep breaths, ignoring the pain. Then he began to climb the cliff, walking up it and pulling himself up hand over hand. Halfway up, he thought he was going to fall back as the wrenched knee buckled. But he recovered, hanging there while he took another deep breath, and resumed the climb.

Fifteen feet wasn't much, but it seemed an eternity before he reached the top and the old man grabbed his hand, helping him over.

"I knew y' could do it, young feller," said the old

man, who didn't look anything at all like Burt McAfee. He was a prospector, rock hammer stuck through a rope belt that held up torn jeans. Raider recognized Dutch Schaeffer's Colt .31 on the other hip.

"Thanks, mister," he said, his senses swimming as he lay back against the slope. An old Henry repeating rifle was propped against a boulder. "You saved my life."

"Mebbe. Come on, we ain't outa this yet."

He turned away, gathering his rope and retrieving his rifle. Raider drew several more deep breaths and stood as the old man came back.

"Do you have a horse? Or a mule?"

"Fer what?" he asked suspiciously.

"I've got to get to Coffin Canyon," Raider answered.

"Y' ain't never gonna make it stove up the way y' are. Best come with me 'n' rest up t' my place fer a few days afore you try anything foolish like climbin' a mountain on foot."

Raider knew the old man was right. "How far is your place?"

"Not far. Not more'n a mile. Jes' foller me."

Using the Henry's stock as support, the old man started to make his way down the slope. After a moment, he looked around impatiently.

"Come on, young feller."

Suspecting that this was still a dream, Raider managed to get to his feet and started to slide down the slope after the old man. Afterward, he could not remember the details of the descent, or how he finally reached the prospector's cabin. Several times he fell, and the old man had to take his arm and help him. He hurt more and more, but the old man would not let him dawdle.

"Come on!" he kept saying, turning around. "We ain't got all day."

They reached the bottom of the canyon. Somehow, Raider managed to stumble along after the old man, holding on to the tail of a mule. For a time, he was riding the mule, his long legs almost scraping the ground. For a time, he lay across the mule's back, the animal's bony spine digging into his belly. And then a cool cloth touched his forehead, bathed his face.

Raider opened his eyes to see an angel bending over him. He blinked, but the beautiful face remained surrounded by a golden halo.

"Am I dead?" he asked.

The angel laughed, a surprisingly human sound, and Raider tried to smile. Then the cloth covered his eyes again and gentle fingers began to undo the buttons of his shirt. He wiggled his toes; his boots had already been removed, as had his gun belt. He raised himself on first one shoulder and then the other, ignoring the bursts of fire, as her fingers tugged. And then she began to undo his buckle, open his trousers.

Aware that lust did not exist in heaven, Raider knew that this was a dream. The angel drew his trousers down from his hips, exposing his nakedness. He felt a stirring in his cock and heard her laugh again as she worked his trousers off his ankles.

She touched his cock.

CHAPTER FOUR

Doc Weatherbee followed Madame Helena von Dorf Coffin up the grand staircase of the Virginia House and into a corridor thickly carpeted and lined with cut crystal wall sconces. An Indian woman in stiffly starched maid's apron and two long black pigtails was coming out of the suite Cee-Cee Coffin's late-life love indicated, but Doc scarcely noticed the serving woman. His eyes were fixed on the singular movement of Madame Helena's bustle.

"I really hope I'm not inconveniencing you, Doctor," she said, turning around and giving Doc a smile that she had long ago sharpened until one slash would let her get away with inconveniencing any man who had two good eyes in his head.

"I'm glad to be of service, Mrs. Coffin."

"I just don't know what could be wrong with my little Zelzah," she said, ushering Doc into an ornate and overstuffed sitting room in which red plush vied with marble for attention at every hand. But Madame Helena did not stop, sweeping into the smaller of two adjoining bedrooms. It was twice as large as Doc's own overfurnished room, meaning that it approached the average bunkhouse in roominess.

"At first she says it's her stomach," said Madame Helena, "and then it's her head, until I don't know what."

Zelzah sat up in bed when they came in. She was wearing a peach-colored bed wrap that did nothing to hide her charms, even though there was an extra layer of nightgown underneath. She was hardly what Doc

29

would call a little girl; he swallowed and would have bitten his cigar in half if he hadn't dumped it downstairs.

The girl in the bed, who pouted when she saw that the visitor was a well-dressed gentleman, had a figure that rivaled her mother's, although perhaps a bit less mature. Her swaddled bosom and her waist were smaller than Madame Helena's, but her hair was the same brilliant auburn. And her small nose had the same up-turn at the end.

"And who is this?" Zelzah demanded sharply, her manner signifying that she, too, was used to having her own way.

"Dear child, I've brought you a doctor," said her mother, hovering at the side of the bed.

"Not that she needs one," said an older girl at the far side of the room, tossing her head. She dropped her needlework on the love seat and stood. "There's not a thing wrong with her that the backside of a hairbrush applied to her backside wouldn't cure!"

"Now, Moravia, let us be ladylike," said her mother reprovingly. "We don't want the doctor to get the wrong idea, now do we?"

There was a hint of menace in her words, and Moravia subsided, turning away. She was tall, as slender as her sister, but her striking long hair was a dark glossy brown. Her face revealed her kinship to the other two women in the room.

Doc felt himself flushing as he reached to pick up Zelzah's wrist, the girl submitting with a shrug. The blatant sexuality of the girls, and of their mother, bothered him. He almost wished that Raider were here in his place. But he could understand how CeeCee had succumbed to the charms of the generously endowed Madame Helena.

"Exactly what seems to be the matter?" he asked, faking a professional manner as he counted the girl's pulse. Her flesh was warm under his fingers, and her heart was racing a bit. A light sheen coated her forehead, but that might have been as much the fault of the weather as of a fever.

Zelzah stuck her full lower lip out in a pout. "I just don't feel well."

"It's her stomach," said Moravia, coyly emphasizing the last word.

Doc reached beneath the comforter and pressed the girl's side, feeling for a swelling and watching for any indication of pain. There was none.

"Does that hurt?"

"No . . . yes!" she said. "Oh, don't do that again!"

"That was your lip," said Doc dryly, looking at Madame Helena. "There really doesn't seem to be anything wrong with her."

"But I'm feeling all out of sorts," Zelzah protested. "Really, I am!"

Madame Helena excused herself and withdrew, and as soon as the door closed, Moravia burst out, "Don't listen to her! She's just trying to get out of going to the opera tonight, Doctor."

"Oh, you hush!" said Zelzah hotly, glaring back at her sister. "As if you didn't have to be dragged away from that silly Doyle Mendoza you were planning to meet tonight!"

"Well," returned Moravia, clearly angry at her own misfortune, "if you hadn't been caught with that dimwit Lloyd Hargrove behind the summerhouse, neither one of us would be here!"

Zelzah could not answer the last charge. "I surely don't know why she even cares, what with her sneaking off every afternoon for her 'ride.' I'll bet it's some ride!"

At first Doc was embarrassed by the sisters' squabbling, but he listened. He was learning more about the Coffin family in five minutes than he had picked up in three weeks, although he wasn't at all sure that it was relevant to his present problems.

Moravia stood and stretched languidly. "You can't

blame mother," she said. "Just look what she married this time."

"Isn't that the truth!" said Zelzah. "That man is as loony as a jackrabbit."

And then the girl turned to Doc, reached out, and caught his hand. "Please, don't give me away, Doctor! I just can't bear the thought of sitting through another opera—the last time she dragged us to one, in Denver, I thought I'd die before I got away."

"You're asking me to lie?" he said sternly.

"It's not such a terrible lie," said the girl. "Just convince Mama that I need to stay in bed. Then when she goes off, I can get up—she's going to one of those late dinners, which means she won't be back until all hours. Please, Doctor? I'd be ever so grateful."

Doc swallowed, and at that moment, Madame Helena returned. He turned to her in relief.

"Well, Doctor?" she asked anxiously. "Is my little Zelzah all right?"

"It seems to be a touch of stomach disorder, madame," said Doc. "However, I can't be certain—I'm told there have been several cases of sefelningitis in the territory. The symptoms are very much like those of a minor upset at the early stages."

"Oh, dear!" Madame Helena wrung her hands. "It sounds serious!"

"It doesn't have to be, if caught in time. Hot epsom salts baths help a great deal. The patient should soak for an hour, with the tub covered with sheets to keep the heat in, and then have an hour out. Alternate the baths with absolute bed rest."

"I'll cancel my plans to attend the opera—"

"No, that won't be necessary. But I would suggest that you have the hotel's physician look in on her this evening. Bed rest is the most important part of the treatment, however, so on no account should she be up for the next twenty-four hours."

Doc gave Madame Helena his most sincere gaze,

watching to see if she swallowed his line. In the corner, Moravia was trying to muffle laughter, and behind the madame, Zelzah glared fearfully. If looks could kill, he was destined to join the dead very shortly.

"I would rather have you continue the treatment," said Mrs. Coffin, her eyes fluttering. "I mean, you seem to know the proper course to follow."

"That would not be possible, Madame. I'm sorry."

"Oh, please, Doctor! I beg you to reconsider."

"I have an engagement," he said firmly. "I may not return until very late."

"But what if the hotel's doctor doesn't know about this scfufelning-itis, doctor? You know how ill-educated so many of these back country doctors are. I beg you . . ."

He sighed and pretended to surrender. "Very well, I'll look in before I leave, and again when I return if it isn't too late."

"Oh, thank you!" said Madame Helena, escorting him to the door of the suite. As he left the girls' bedroom, he saw Zelzah stick out her tongue. "Believe me, I do appreciate this, Doctor."

"I'll do what I can," said Doc, and he made his escape, hurrying to his own room. Madame Helena von Dorf Coffin was a veritable juggernaut of a woman, and he felt as if he had just leaped off a railroad trestle before a speeding locomotive came tearing across.

Doc sighed and tried to shake off the pessimism that had dogged him as the weeks slipped by with no results in the current investigation. One of these days a nastily worded wire would come from Wagner in Chicago, demanding to know what he was doing to justify the steadily mounting expenses of his stay in this city. Things would have to break soon.

He wondered if Raider was having any more luck with the ore shipment as he brought out his journal and proceeded to bring it up to date—mentioning the meeting with the indomitable Mrs. Coffin. Everything went into the journal, no matter how trivial or seemingly irrelevant.

Putting away the journal, he coded the message to Wagner—from memory, since it was the same one he had been sending for days now—and took it down to the Western Union office. A barefoot urchin dogged his steps from the hotel to the telegraph office, demanding money. The boy was still there when Doc came out.

"Go away, boy!" said Doc, irritated, digging a copper from his pocket. The lad snatched it out of midair and fell back. But when Doc came out of the barber shop an hour later, he spotted the same boy hanging around the end of the block. Nuisance, he thought grumpily, and he dismissed him from his mind.

Shortly before dinner, he knocked on the door of the Coffin suite. It was answered by Moravia, who grinned when she saw him.

"Come in," she said saucily. "If you care nothing for your life, that is."

"You managed to wiggle out of the opera, too?" asked Doc.

"Someone has to stay and watch dear sister," said Moravia, leading him to the bedroom. "Dear Mama, of course, could never give up her evening to care for her daughters."

Zelzah was sitting up in bed, the covers pushed down and the bed wrap thrown aside, exposing her charms beneath the wispy nightgown. She glared at Doc when he came into the room.

"Bastard!"

"Tut tut," said Doc, stopping a safe distance away in case the girl decided to throw something. "I can still order those alternating hot baths for you."

"You try it, and I'll rip your heart out of your black hide!" said Zelzah. "I want out of this prison!"

"Tomorrow," said Doc. "After lunch. I'll look in on the patient again later, Miss Coffin."

"Oh, our name isn't Coffin," said Moravia, escorting

him back to the door while a book crashed against the wall of the bedroom. "It's Riley—Papa was Mama's first husband. Of course, there have been so many since Papa, I'm not sure I remember them all."

"Oh?" That was interesting. Doc made a mental note to begin a discreet inquiry into the background of Madame Helena Coffin. "Well, I'll look in again later, if it isn't too late."

Moravia studied Doc closely, clinging to the open door; suddenly he felt a rush of sexual heat, and he beat a hasty retreat. He could not say for sure that the girl had given him the come-on, but he certainly did not intend to mix business with pleasure. Besides, she was only a child!

When Doc returned, just past midnight, to make his promised late call, however, the door was opened by Madame Helena herself. Doc's eyebrows and jaw went in opposite directions as he took in the thin silk dressing gown that clung to her voluptuous curves like a glove. Suddenly he knew that she had nothing on beneath the gown.

"Uh . . ." he said, stammering, "I promised to . . . uh . . . look in on Zelzah . . ."

"Oh, she's been asleep for hours," said Madame Helena, catching his arm. "But come in, Doctor, please. Join me in a nightcap."

She didn't quite jerk him into the suite, but suddenly the door was closed behind Doc's back, and Madame Helena was leading him toward a sofa. The door to the girls' room was closed, but another door opposite stood open, revealing the bedroom that belonged to the mistress of the house. . . .

CHAPTER FIVE

Raider looked down at the girl, who had begun to stroke him gently between the thighs, and groaned. He fell back and closed his eyes to keep the room from spinning.

"Honey," he said, "I don't for one minute believe you're real. But even if this isn't a dream, you might as well give up. All the angels in heaven could come down in their birthday suits and it wouldn't help one bit."

The girl laughed, a liquid trill that sent shivers racing along Raider's spine. For a moment longer the touch remained, light and gentle as her fingers traced his sexual organs. He felt fire as his cock tried to respond, but at this moment he was too far gone.

The touch disappeared, and the girl arranged a blanket over his nakedness. Raider dozed for a time and then woke to see the old prospector at one side of the bed, the girl at the other.

"Ye better sit up, mister," said the old man, "so's we can git a good look at yer."

Somehow he struggled to an upright position, sitting hunched over while the two studied the network of scars that traced his back. Raider winced as the old man touched the entrance and exit wounds of the bullet. He could feel the fever in his flesh.

"Infectin'," said the old man. "Amity, git some water hotted up so's we can clean it out."

The girl turned away. So her name was Amity. Raider looked around at the prospector.

"Do you have a name?"

"Happens I do," he said sourly. "Most folks do. Some folks don't pry, lessen they interduces themselves first."

"Fair enough—ow!" Raider gasped as the old man prodded at the wound again. "I'm John O'Toole."

"Zachariah Gilchrist. Zach to most."

Raider ground his teeth together as the prodding and poking went on. He looked around the cabin, trying to distract his attention from his miseries. He was on a narrow bed in the corner. The head of the bed was perhaps five feet from a stove, where Amity poked at a fire. A pan of water was heating on the stove's top.

Across the room, a tattered hanging covered a door, probably into a lean-to addition. The front door and the window stood open to the breeze, to the flies that buzzed loudly in the somnolent summer afternoon, and to the sunlight. Dust motes danced everywhere.

There was a table, a rude, homemade thing, like the bed and the other articles of furniture. On the table were fifteen or so silver ingots. Raider was sure they would prove to have the marking of the Coffin Queen.

Amity brought the hot water and a reasonably clean rag and bent to dab at the two wounds with the cloth. Raider winced again at the contact but kept from crying out by clenching his teeth.

"Scabbin' over," said the girl. "We better break it off, Zach."

"You do it," said the prospector sourly. Raider wondered at the relationship between them as Amity brought a razor-thin boning knife and set to work as though the surgery were something she performed every day. Tears coursed from his eyes and ran down his cheeks before she finished, but he still made not a sound.

"Oughta be catterized," said Amity critically.

"It'll wait," Raider said hastily. "At least until I get back to Coffin Canyon."

"Like hell!" said Amity, matter of factly. "You wait till you get back to Coffin, it'll be all down your arm, mister. 'Course, that'll save the sawbones trouble—all he'll have t' do is amputate it. At the neck."

Zach chuckled. "Better listen to her, Mister O'Toole. Amity's right good at doctorin'."

Not waiting for the go-ahead from her patient, Amity stuck a poker into the fire. Suddenly weak, Raider lay back down. He wasn't afraid of most mortal men, but the thought of the red-hot poker against his flesh was enough to make him quaver.

While the poker heated, Zach left the cabin for a minute. Amity drew up a chair and sat down, her hands folded between her legs. She wore cut-off jeans and a cotton shirt; men's clothing, the sleeves of the shirt rolled up and held with bright green garters.

"Is Zach your father?" he asked.

"Naw." Amity shook her head. "Zach and my grandpap was partners—he took me in when grandpap died. I was just a leetle one then."

"You been living here ever since?"

"Here, an' a few other places. Wherever Zach plants his claim. Don't make much difference—one place is about the same as another."

Raider looked toward the door. It was late afternoon; suddenly he thought of Doc and struggled to sit up. Amity leaned forward and pushed him with one hand, and he fell back again, unable to stand against her strength.

"I've got to get to Coffin Canyon!" he said desperately. "I've got to tell 'em about the ambush."

"I figger they'll know soon enough, when the silver don't git where it's supposed to be," said Amity. "No point killin' yourself over somethin' you can't help nohow."

Before Raider could argue further, Zach came back into the cabin. He carried a stone jug, and brought it over to Raider, uncorking it.

"Better have a swaller er two of this, O'Toole," he said. "Help with the pain."

Raider cupped the jug and held it to his lips, and liquid lightning trickled into his throat. He coughed, spraying Zach's clothing.

"Jesus! That's pure swamp water!"

Zach cackled. "Sure makes a feller sit up an' think twice, don't it? Git it from an Injun down on the Truckee Flats. Take another swaller—you'll need it."

Raider did as Zach suggested, swallowing cautiously. The amber liquid hit bottom and lay there a moment, and then a series of bombs went off, one after another, that left him gasping for breath. He hardly noticed when Amity told him to turn over and hold on to the bedposts.

"You hold still, or I'll tie you down," said the girl.

"Do it 'n' be done with it, damn it!" said Raider.

He tensed, back arched, as the girl inserted the tip of the poker into the entrance and exit wounds. Raider suppressed a scream, his knuckles whitening and his buttocks tensing as the hot iron cauterized the wound. The pain was terrible, but it lasted only a minute, and then his shoulder went numb.

"It'll leave a scar, but nobody'll notice with all the marks you got there already," said Amity, swabbing the twin burns with foul-smelling ointment. "What do they do, John O'Toole? Use you for target practice?"

"It's been tried a time or two," said Raider, sighing as the pain ebbed.

"You must have a passel of enemies," said Amity.

"I've got to get back to Coffin Canyon," he said anxiously.

"Mebbe tomorrow. We'll see then."

Raider sighed; the sigh turned into a bubbling exhalation as he fell into sleep.

It was night, and pitch dark. He blinked and turned over, groaning as the injured shoulder took his weight for a moment. He could see nothing but faint afterflashes in the darkness that were his eyes playing tricks.

A hand touched his leg. Raider stopped breathing as the bed creaked beneath the weight of the girl. She leaned across his legs, and a warm, moist tongue began to work its way up the inside of his thigh.

"Amity?"

"Shut up, John O'Toole. Yer dreamin'."

Raider moaned and reached to stop her. "You're wastin' your time. I'm two-thirds dead, and the other third dead tired."

Amity ignored his protest, her tongue working up one thigh and down the other. Raider's still-limp cock was slowly engulfed in the warm cavern of her mouth, caressed by her curling tongue. She nipped him, forcing a groan.

"Christ, stop, girl!" He tried to push her away. "You'll kill me!"

"Then you ain't much of a man," she said.

And even as Raider protested, his cock rose, slowly and by its own volition, brought to life by the girl's expert teasing. Raider was shocked to feel himself stiffening, becoming engorged, becoming large.

"Jesus!" he muttered, settling back, his hands curled into fists. "Ahhhh, Jesus!"

Amity could no longer fit the whole of his huge member into her mouth. She worked up and down its enormous length with quick, sharp bites—and stopped, as suddenly as she had begun.

Raider opened his eyes again, aware that he was burning hard. His groin ached; and now he could see shadows in the room. Amity had stopped only to remove her shirt and step out of her jeans. Her breasts were small, golden apples crowned with dark areolae that enticed as she climbed on top of him, straddling him.

"Where's Zach?" he demanded.

"Dead drunk, and dead to the world," she replied, humping tentatively. "What the hell difference does it make? Zach minds his business and I mind mine, John O'Toole. He don't own me."

Raider sucked in a sharp breath as she tightened her cunt muscles against him. "Then why do you stay here?" he asked.

Amity shrugged. "I guess I figger I owe him. Zach raised me when I had no kinfolk to take me in. If I was to leave, he'd fall in a hole someplace, mebbe die without no one knowin'."

Raider reached to take her hips in his strong hands, but he lacked the strength to pull her forward. Amity rose up and reached down with one hand to gently guide his cock into her body. It was a tight fit; he gasped again, for she was not wet enough to make the entrance easy.

"Ahhh, yer a big man, John O'Toole," she said, sighing with what might have been happiness. "Big as they come, ain't yer?"

Raider didn't answer; there was no answer that a self-respecting man could give to that question. Amity began to rock, at first slowly and then faster, with each swing sliding a bit farther down on his cock. And then she gasped, seating herself all the way, and straightened, back arched and fingertips on her thighs while she drew a slow breath.

"I got it!" she cried in triumph. "I got it!"

And with that, Amity began to move up and down, throwing her weight against Raider. He gasped and cursed and cried out in sudden pain, but she ignored him, rocking faster and faster, driving him deeper and deeper into her loins each time she came down.

"Oh, shit!" said the girl, coming. "Ahhhh, sweet Jesus!"

Orgasm didn't slow the ride, although a long shudder arched Amity's back spasmodically. She pumped a dozen more times, with great force, and then came down onto all fours, still impaled on Raider's cock.

"Jesus," he said softly, as Amity rested her head on

his chest. He was still engorged; he hadn't come. He thrust up, once, and she began to move with him. The pains and aches dimmed, overshadowed by the sensations wrought in Raider's cock and his loins by the sex-hungry girl.

He caught her arms, tried to force her over, wanting to mount her; but his body failed him. Amity continued to ride him as he said, "Oh, Christ!" over and over, monotonously. She began to pant, moaning aloud as she came again and again, as she tried to force him to climax.

And then she slipped off, to lie beside him, holding his throbbing cock in her hand. Somehow Raider managed to turn onto his side, and Amity guided him into her cunt again. He began to move, although she was still in control. She tightened her cunt, skewering herself on his thrusting cock.

Raider found strength in some unknown reservoir and drove into the girl until both knew that he was close to exploding. He ignored the aches and pains and protests of his muscles as he reached his arms around Amity and began to drive violently. In a dozen strokes, he felt his belly tightening with the need to explode . . . and a dozen strokes later, his guts melted, and he came deep into her cunt with a gush of warmth.

Amity sighed as Raider held to her a moment longer; then she pulled away and slipped from the bed. A silly grin settled over Raider's face as his eyes closed, and he drifted into a dreamless sleep.

It was morning when he woke, stiffer than ever when he tried to turn over. There was no sign of either Amity or Zach, and after several minutes of struggle, he managed to sit up and reach for his pants. The girl came into the cabin as he tried to pull them over his feet.

"What do you think yer doin'?" she demanded.

"I've got to go," he said.

"You ain't gonna make it outa the canyon."

"Maybe not, but I'm gonna try."

Amity shook her head at his stubbornness, but she helped Raider dress. Pulling on his Middleton boots was sheer torture; if she hadn't been there, he would have given up and started out barefoot. But at last he was ready, although he leaned on the table when he did stand.

"Tell Zach I said thanks." There didn't seem to be any need to offer to pay for what they had done, with the silver Zach had salvaged from the ambush. In normal circumstances, Raider would have mentioned it, but now he was willing to let it pass.

"You take care of yourself, John O'Toole," said Amity.

He managed a wry grin and took a hesitant step, giving up the support of the table. Three more steps took him to the door; he stood there a moment, leaning against the jamb while he breathed in the morning air. His stomach rumbled with hunger, but Raider ignored its complaint, intent on getting back to the Coffin Queen.

He sighed, took a single step out of the cabin, and fell flat on his face.

CHAPTER SIX

Doc returned to his room in the Virginia House wearier than he had been an hour before. He shook his head in amazement at the redoubtable Helena von Dorf Coffin, wondering if Junius and his brothers had any notion of their stepmama's extracurricular activities. But, as Madame Helena had said, "I'm fond of my husband, Doctor, don't you ever mistake me on that. But a woman does need a little change from time to time, and Cee-Cee, bless him, is slowing down."

Madame Helena showed no sign of slowing. Doc's testicles ached as he unlocked his door and entered his room, kicking a yellow telegram envelope across the throw rug. He paused to strike a match to a lamp and then bent down with a smothered groan to retrieve the message.

Someone had written "Received 6:40 P.M." across the envelope. That was ten minutes after Doc had gone out for the evening. He ran his finger under the flap and unfolded the form. The message was short and simple, carefully packed into the ten-word minimum:

SHIPMENT AMBUSHED STOP RECOV-
ERED SEVEN BODIES STOP NO SIGN
O'TOOLE STOP PRESUMED DEAD STOP

The telegram was signed "Junius Coffin." Doc read it three times and then began to curse, pouring out a low, voluble stream of anger against the men who had done the deed, against Raider for having gotten himself killed. Or taken prisoner. Although the latter didn't seem likely.

The worst of Doc's anger was against himself, for feeling such a sudden surge of grief for his troublesome partner. He crumpled the telegram, fingers working the paper until it tore; then he threw it into a spittoon. Not watching to see it land, he brought his carpetbag out of the sideboard and began to pack.

It was two in the morning when he finished and took a last look around the room to be sure he had forgotten nothing. All thought of sleep had left him. The weariness caused by his exercise with Helena Coffin was forgotten. The journal and the code book were in the carpetbag, buried beneath his clothing. On top, where Doc could grab it quickly, was his Colt Diamondback .38; that was clear evidence of his upset state of mind, for Doc ordinarily avoided guns as though they were poison. He preferred using his wits as a weapon against the usual run of miscreants whom his Pinkerton duties brought him against.

There was no sign of the night clerk when Doc went down to the desk, but he found the man sleeping in the office. The clerk almost jumped out of his clothes when Doc kicked the pedestal of his swivel chair, spinning him around.

"Whazzit—"

"I'm checking out," said Doc. "Prepare my bill. And I'll want a rig."

"Now?" The clerk stood, hitching up his pants and adjusting his suspenders as he eyed the clock on the wall. "It's two in the mornin', mister. The livery ain't open this time of night."

"Then open it," said Doc coldly. "You're wasting my time."

The clerk eyed Doc and decided that dude or not,

he had better do what Doc said. Ten minutes later Doc met the livery stable's owner in front of his barn, that worthy wearing bedroom slippers that flopped as he scuffed through the manure in the yard and pants with the fly open over his red underwear. The man cursed when Doc told him he wanted to leave the rig in the town of Washoe.

"If'n I gotta send a man fer my rig, that'll cost yer exter, mister."

"Just get on with it," said Doc sharply.

Two or three of the more disreputable saloons still showed lights when Doc drove out of the stable ten minutes later, but the honest citizens were in their beds, except perhaps along Millionaire's Row. The streets were empty. Doc whipped up the horse, a spavined nag that should have been sent to the glue factory years ago. The wheels rattled loudly and the rig heeled dangerously far over when Doc took a curve at too great a speed. The liveryman had clearly unloaded his worst equipment on the unwelcome late-night customer.

But the rig held together, and the horse managed to stay alive for the two hours it took to make the run down Mount Davidson to the hamlet of Washoe. Dawn was still a faint hope in the eastern skies when Doc rolled into the yard of the farmer who was boarding Judith.

He pounded up the porch steps and knocked loudly, until the farmer appeared, carrying a lantern. The man scowled when he spoke through the door but opened it when Doc identified himself and put an old cap-and-ball Dragoon on the hall table.

"Sorry to bother you at this time," said Doc, "but I need my wagon."

"Runnin' from the law?" asked the farmer suspiciously. "Not that it's any er my business."

He led the way to the barn. Judith pricked up her ears and uttered a sound at Doc's familiar smell, then brayed when he patted her muzzle.

"Hello, old girl," he said fondly. "We have work to do—that damn fool Raider's gone and got himself into another fix."

Judith tossed her head as though agreeing with Doc's opinion about his partner. And twenty minutes later, after settling his bill, Doc and Judith were on their way to Coffin Canyon.

Perched on the seat of the Studebaker wagon, Doc felt comfortable for the first time in three weeks. The brightly painted canvas sides flapped in the morning breeze as the sun broke over the eastern peaks. The valleys, canyons, and roads were still in darkness, however, and a few fading stars still dotted the western sky.

"Dumb bastard!" said Doc softly, as Judith plodded patiently onward. "This time he's gone and got himself killed!"

Judith made good time, for a mule, as though she understood the urgency of their mission. But basically a mule has one speed, which slowed as the road into the mountains grew steeper. Doc gently urged her on.

"Come on, old girl. Raider needs us."

He stopped once, just long enough to hang Judith's feedbag, and then clambered back onto the seat. As the hours passed, Doc's worry increased, although he tried to reassure himself by remembering the many times that Raider had been in tight spots and managed to wiggle out of them, even if not always with a whole hide. He refused to accept the last two words of Junius Coffin's telegram.

There were no towns along the road from Washoe to Coffin Canyon, and few farms or ranches. On the flats, Judith could make two or three miles an hour, but climbing into the mountains, that was halved. It was less than thirty miles, but when the late summer darkness fell, they were still three hours or more from their goal.

Doc was hungry. He cursed himself for not buying sandwiches from the farmer and then remembered a tin of English biscuits he had stowed in the wagon a while back. The cookies were stale, but they filled his stomach; he refilled his canteen in a mountain stream, jumping down and climbing back into the seat without stopping Judith.

Blast it all! Nothing had gone right with this case, from the moment he and Raider had stopped at the Denver office. Doc had sat around Virginia City for three weeks, wasting time—although he had met Helena Coffin and her daughters, he amended his last thought. That meeting had not been wasted, although it was doubtful that it would be of much use in solving the problems besetting Helena's stepsons.

He sighed and spoke soothing words to Judith, which the mule accepted as her just due. The news that Raider was missing could be either good or bad, although Doc could see no reason for his being taken prisoner—unless the bandits knew of his Pinkerton connections.

Which would mean that either Junius Coffin or his brothers had been speaking out of turn. Or perhaps Raider had gotten away but was trailing the outlaws back to their hideout. Doc would not accept that Raider was dead; not without a body.

"Heyaw, Judith! Let's go, girl!"

It was twenty minutes past midnight when Doc rolled into the town of Coffin Canyon and drove Judith into the livery stable's yard. The town was silent, the houses dark, but the offices of the Coffin Queen mine blazed with light. He unhitched Judith and let her fill her stomach with water; then he bedded her down in an empty stall with a ration of grain. She had done Doc proud this day.

No one came out to see what Doc was doing as he took care of his mule and wagon, nor did anyone appear as he hurried toward the Queen, the Diamondback stuck into his belt. A hardcase stood outside Junius Coffin's office, eying Doc with suspicion. But he took his name inside, and thirty seconds later, Doc was in the company of the brothers. Junius sat behind his desk, Jasper, the middle brother, was on a leather sofa, while Jonathan, the youngest, perched on the edge of a straight-backed chair. Jonathan was well on his way to getting drunk. He held himself carefully, as though afraid to lean back or bend forward any farther. A water tumbler of whisky stood on a small table by his elbow.

Jasper had the look of a middle-aged clerk, tufts of graying hair sticking up on the sides of his head where he had run ink-stained fingers through it. Jonathan glared at Doc as Junius made the introductions.

"A fine mess this is," he said. "We're paying Pinkerton's a damn good amount of money for protection, and what happens? With your man along, the same as happened to every other shipment—stolen! Goddamn it, why?"

"Settle down, Jonathan," said Junius sharply.

"Bullshit!" said Jonathan. "I want to know what the hell Pinkerton's is going to do!"

"Everything possible," said Doc, scowling. He had dozed from time to time during the day, but he was dead on his feet and not about to take shit from a pipsqueak like Jonathan Coffin. He worked the fingers of his right hand, and Junius caught the move. He jumped into the breach.

"Did you learn anything at all in Virginia City?"

"Just that Coffin seems to be the most hated name in the Comstock," said Doc. "I'd say there were about thirty-five hundred suspects in Virginia City alone, just counting those who publicly say they've no use for the lot of you."

"Who the hell do you think you are?" cried Jonathan. "You can't come in here and insult us!"

"Shut up!" said Junius, growing angry. "Jonathan, if you can't keep your mouth shut, get out!"

Jonathan subsided, taking a healthy swig from his tumbler as Jasper clucked his tongue in despair. He spoke.

"What are you going to do now, Weatherbee?"

"Right now," said Doc, "I'm going to find a bed and fall into it for about eight hours. I haven't had any sleep for the last thirty-six or so—I've been on the road since two this morning. Yesterday morning," he corrected, looking at a wall clock. "After that, I'll check out the scene of the ambush."

"You can stay at my house," said Junius.

"I'd rather check in at the hotel," said Doc. "Unless you're ready to spill it that I'm with Pinkerton's. There's no point to that yet."

"You're probably right." Junius stood, obviously tired and looking a good deal older than he had in Denver three weeks before. He followed Doc out of the office, where the latter turned on the guard.

"You haven't seen me," said Doc sharply.

"That's right, Rollins," said Junius. "If anyone should ask, you never heard of Weatherbee."

Rollins shrugged without a word, and Doc left, saying good night to Junius. He found the hotel, a two-story frame structure, and found a light at the desk, but there was no sign of a night clerk. At last he signed the register and took a key from the rack. And five minutes later, not bothering to unpack his carpetbag or hang his suit on the hook on the back of the door, not even bothering to change his underwear for his nightshirt, Doc rolled into the bed.

He closed his eyes, but sleep eluded him for several minutes. He rolled over with a moan, pummeled the pillow, and stared into the darkness at the ceiling overhead.

Raider couldn't be dead! Goddamn it, if his partner had gone and gotten himself killed, he'd . . .

The absurdity of the thought struck Doc. For a moment longer, he lay in the darkness with his eyes open. And then blessed sleep captured him.

CHAPTER SEVEN

Raider thought he was going to black out as his chin hit the ground and jarred the still-tender tooth. Then he felt Amity's knees against his ribs as the girl tried to turn him over, and he groaned. Somehow he managed to roll onto his side and then rise to a sitting position, leaning against her.

"Yer a damn fool, John O'Toole!" the girl said hotly. "Now will you listen to sense? You ain't gonna be fit t' travel fer at least a couple of days."

"Dammit, I can't wait that long," said Raider stubbornly. "You'll have to go to Coffin Canyon for me."

She laughed harshly. "Not likely. I got better things t' do than go gallivantin' aroun'."

bornly. "You'll have to go to Coffin Canyon for me." set. Her eyes blazed with a strange fire. He wondered what Amity had against Coffin Canyon—or its inhabitants. He considered arguing the point but decided against it.

"Zach will have to go, then," he said.

"Mebbe." Amity shrugged. "You can ask him when he gits back. If he's a mind to, he might."

"Help me stand."

Raider reached for her hand as Amity muttered something under her breath that sounded like "Asshole!" But she helped him to his feet and then into the cabin. He leaned against the doorjamb after negotiating the single step, his head spinning, and said a silent curse or two of his own. But he knew Amity was right —for life itself, he couldn't have made it fifty yards from the cabin. The fever that had come with the infected shoulder wound had drained him of strength. Sleep, and food, would restore him, but he was stuck here for at least the next two or three days.

"Help me back to bed."

" 'Bout time you said somethin' sensible," said Amity.

She was strong. His face was beaded with perspiration, and he felt feverish when they finally crossed the short distance to the bed. The fever fire seemed localized in his shoulder, and he moaned as he collapsed across the straw tick. Amity cursed as she saw a dark stain spread across his shirt.

"Yer bleedin' again," she said, rolling him onto his side to undo his buttons. "I'll have t' change the dressin', ya damn fool."

"Water first," said Raider, his mouth suddenly dry. "God, I'm burnin' up!"

She brought him a dipper of water, holding his head up so he could drink. Then Amity managed to undress him again, Raider unable to help. By the time she had changed the dressing, he was in a fevered doze, moaning as she pulled the blood-soaked cloth away from the wound and moaning again as he relived the ambush. He didn't know when she finished and arranged the blanket over his trembling body . . .

Doc opened his eyes to the heat of midday. The sun fell across his cheek as he lay on the edge of the sprung bed, only a foot away from the window.

He blinked a time or two, not remembering where he was; then he sat up with a curse and reached for the watch he had placed on the battered bureau that was the room's only article of furniture apart from the bed.

Almost one-thirty. Wide awake, Doc moaned at the thought of lost hours and wasted time. By now he should have been at the site of the ambush.

He stood, scratching his ribs, and then used the chamber pot, yawning widely. Bladder pressure had wakened him; otherwise, he'd still be asleep.

Feeling grimy, he checked the water pitcher on the bureau, but it was empty except for several dead flies and a large dust ball. He checked his blue tricot suit, but it would never be the same again. Wishing he had time for a bath, Doc dressed in black broadcloth. It would be more practical for climbing around the side of the mountain, even if it wasn't his preferred stylish cut. As an afterthought, he slipped the Diamondback into an inside pocket. Then he went downstairs, to find a middle-aged woman behind the desk.

"You must be Weatherbee," she said, looking up from the register. "You stayin' long?"

"I don't know," said Doc. "A few days, anyhow."

"Room's dollar and a half a day, eight dollars a week." She brushed a graying curl back from her face as though trying to be coquettish as she studied Doc. Even unbathed and unshaven, he was a handsome specimen. "Fifteen a week, if you want breakfast an' supper."

"Any chance of lunch?" asked Doc, producing a National Bank Note as he glanced toward the closed dining room. "I'll pay for a week, but I'll take the meals extra."

"Dining room closes at one," replied the woman suspiciously, snapping the bank note in her hands. For a moment Doc thought she was going to smell the ink. Gold was the preferred currency in all of the West, but gold tended to weigh down the pockets. At last she bent beneath the desk and came up with two silver dollars in change.

"Any other eating places in town?" he asked.

"The Chink's, down the street," said the woman, screwing up her face at the mention of the competition. "Not that I'd wanna eat there myself."

As he left, Doc reflected that he wasn't at all sure that he wanted to try the hotel's dining room, even though it was the only hotel in Coffin Canyon. However, he had been in boom towns where a customer was as apt to find himself sharing the bed with two or three strangers.

Coffin Canyon was a one-mine town, however, and there was little call for competition. A placard in a window of the hotel announced that this was "A Temperance Establishment," but there were four saloons to take up the slack and slake the thirst of the men who worked the Coffin Queen. The main street was only two blocks long, with a general store, a dry goods emporium and a drug store; Doc made a note to stop in and replenish his stock of a few of the more popular nostrums in his wagon. He had intended to do it in Denver, but there had been no opportunity before receiving the new assignment to help the Coffins.

The restaurant was in the next block; peeling gilt letters on the windows announced "Wong Fat's Eating Restaurant." The noon rush was over, and the place was empty, but Wong Fat himself came rushing out of the back, bowing, his pigtail bobbing, to take Doc's order for four eggs, a steak, and a plate of potatoes. The coffee had whiskers, but when he finished, he felt human. Unwashed, but human. He added a dime tip to the half-dollar for the meal.

The barber shop had a sign that read "Baths 50¢," but Doc resolutely passed it by, tempting though the thought of soaking in hot water might be. Passing the yard of the Queen, he saw Jasper Coffin standing in the door of the office, his hair still rumpled, his vest hanging open, wearing a green eyeshade. He gave no sign of recognizing Doc as the latter passed by, into the yard of the livery stable.

Doc found an elderly one-armed black man in the office. That worthy introduced himself as Constantine Abernathy, the name that matched the sign over the stable.

"Medicine man, huh?" said Mr. Abernathy. "You got any of Dr. Pelham's Arrowroot Tonic?"

"I'm afraid not," said Doc. "I have mostly homeopathic medicines, as well as electric invigorators, magnetic belts, rheumatism bracelets, and the like. Are you married, Mr. Abernathy?"

"Yeah, I guess you could say that," said the liveryman. "If a marriage blessed by the devil is legal."

"Perhaps your wife would like to own Dr. Scott's Electric Flesh Brush," said Doc smoothly, falling into his sales pitch. "The brush quickly produces a beautiful clear skin and imparts new energy·and new life to all who use it daily."

He turned to the wagon and rummaged in a box behind the seat as Abernathy said dubiously, "Well, now, I dunno as I wants my woman to have any more energy. 'Pears to me she's got about as much energy as any normal woman could use in two lifetimes."

Doc came up with a black brush of some molded material, the ornate back displaying a raised arm clenching lightning bolts over the word "ELECTRIC," and below that, a coat of arms formed by a cinched belt with the words "The Germ of All Life Is Electricity" printed on it. He rubbed the bristles across his sleeve and then showed Abernathy how the needle of a small silver compass jumped when brought close to the bristle.

"Proof positive that this is a genuine electric brush," said Doc, "advertised in all the leading periodicals. The compass is free."

"How much might it be?" asked Abernathy, screwup his face in much the manner of the hotel woman as he accepted the brush to examine it.

"Retail price is three dollars, but I'll let you have it for my cost," said Doc. "A dollar fifty—applied against the board for my mule."

"Done!" said Abernathy quickly, as if he were afraid Doc would change his mind. "How long you figger on stayin' ?"

"Several days at least. And I'll want a horse for today—two horses," he said, changing his mind. A horse would get him down to the scene of the ambush more quickly than Judith, and enough hours had been wasted.

The second horse was for Raider. If he could travel. If he weren't dead.

Doc pushed that thought out of his mind while Abernathy saddled the two horses, one a fine sorrel and the other a gray. At the last minute, Doc brought his bedroll from the wagon and then paused to say a word or two to Judith. He made a further stop at the general store, stocking up on the bare essentials in case it should be necessary to camp out for a night or longer.

Then he rode out of town, passing the big house above the main entrance to the mine that belonged to CeeCee Coffin. The boys lived in three houses built to the same plan but decidedly smaller than their father's house.

The first, belonging to Junius, was painted white, with lilacs and rose bushes in the dooryard. The second, Jasper's, was painted a sensible if dull gray, with no flower beds at all. Jasper was the bachelor of the brothers. The third house, Jonathan's, was painted an astonishingly bright yellow, trimmed with white. There were flower beds everywhere, a riot of color. As Doc rode past, Jonathan's wife came out onto the front porch, using her hand as a fan. She glanced his way as she settled into a porch swing, a pretty woman. Remembering her husband's drunken performance in the mine office the night before, Doc felt sorry for her.

The back road down from Coffin Canyon led past several abandoned mine workings. There was nothing to say whether they were part of the Queen or ventures of other men who had tried to cash in on CeeCee Coffin's luck. A road that circled below the town was lined with abandoned houses and other structures, mute evidence that the population had once been much greater. The structures were weather-beaten, unpainted, in the nature of boom town buildings, which were as often as not pulled down to be moved to the next strike.

There was something depressing about the abandoned part of town. Doc was glad to leave it behind. The horses made much better time than Judith could have managed, and much better than the ore wagon, even though he didn't press them. He covered the distance to Graveyard Gap, following instructions given him the night before by Junius Coffin, in half the time the silver shipment had taken.

It was just past six when Doc reached his destination. It was easy to see the tracks of the ambushers and the ruts made by the waiting wagon that had hauled off the silver. Doc studied the latter tracks a moment; then, on foot, he followed them back into the trees.

"By damn!" he said aloud. "A stagecoach! That's how the bastards took the silver away."

Someone must have seen the coach, for the road, although lightly travelled, did have some traffic. The wreck of the ore wagon had been discovered by an itinerant preacher, who had first come on the horses turned loose by the raiders as they grazed alongside the road, their panic forgotten.

The preacher had seen no stagecoach, and no men on horseback; according to Junius, however, there were several trails that led away from the main road farther down the mountain. At least a couple wandered through the canyons and rejoined the main road farther down. One climbed the next mountain, cresting it near the 9,000-foot level—much higher than Coffin Canyon or Virginia City. Doc couldn't see a stagecoach going that way.

The raiders had been careful not to leave clues as to their identity in tossed-aside trash, although the ground among the trees where they had waited was well-chewed by their horses. He gave up and rode on to the place where the wagon had gone off the road. The wreckage was strewn almost to the canyon bottom, although the bodies had been removed and returned to Coffin Canyon. The ore wagon was smashed beyond repair. Doc wondered if it had been rolled off the road after the silver had been unloaded as a last act of vandalism.

Standing at the edge of the road, he studied the canyon bottom and the steep cliffs that rose on the far side. It was a bleak sight. The dark green of the evergreens was hardly a sign of life, scattered as they were among the barren rocks. Raider couldn't have gone down that slope with the wagon. No man could survive that.

Sighing, Doc mounted his horse again. There were still a couple of hours of daylight left, time enough to find the trails, and maybe check out at least one of them for evidence that the bandits had gone that way. Taking Raider with them, he prayed as he rode on.

CHAPTER EIGHT

Doc followed the first trail he found, a mile below the Gap, into a canyon. Darkness quickly caught up with him. He camped beside a stream, unwilling to trust his luck to the treacherous ground.

But he was far from ready for sleep when he stretched out in his bedroll, staring at a spangled heaven that was astonishing testament to God's work. His thoughts were in turmoil as he pondered the fate of his partner.

Doc wasn't a tracker—Raider was far more skilled at finding and following a trail. But he knew the silver had not come over this rough road. Other trails kept leading off into the hills, made by prospectors searching for the elusive El Dorado that CeeCee Coffin had found.

This camp site had seen frequent use. A substantial mound of tin cans rusted under the trees, and several men had carved their names in a massive deadfall.

First light found Doc finishing a scant breakfast; the horses were already saddled. He rode out, and twenty minutes later he found himself back on the main road. He retraced his steps, to make sure the bandits hadn't taken off between here and where he had left the road above; then he headed down the mountain.

The day passed without luck. There were places where the coach could have been driven over the mountain, but Doc missed any sign that might have been left. At last, as evening lowered over the canyons and valleys, he came out onto the flats and spotted the lights of a ranch house a mile away.

He headed that way, toward the first sign of human life since he had left Coffin Canyon. The mountain peaks were still touched by sun as Doc rode into the yard, although the sky to the west was purple-gray and showed the first stars. His coming had been heard; the rancher waited in the door, a shotgun under his arm.

"Name is Weatherbee," said Doc, not dismounting. "I work for the Coffin Queen mine. Perhaps you heard they had another shipment of silver robbed three days ago?"

"Heard nothin'," said the rancher. "Ain't seen nothin', neither—ain't been no strangers rode by, if that's what yer thinkin'."

Doc could see a pair of towheads behind the farmer. The kids strained to hear. "Are there any other ranches in the vicinity?"

The farmer shrugged, not relaxing his hold on the shotgun. "The Double F, 'bout three miles down. Brannigan's, back in Blue Horse Canyon—road leads off t'other side of Blasted Rock. Scourby's, if yer turn off fer Carson City."

Doc eyed the sky. He might just make the Double F, riding full out, before darkness. On the other hand, any band riding down from Coffin Canyon would have to pass by here, if they stuck to the main road. It wasn't likely he'd find out anything more at the next ranch than he knew now.

He touched the brim of his hat. "I'm much obliged. I'd be more grateful if you could suggest a place I might camp for the night."

Greed overcame the farmer's mistrust of strangers. "You can bed down in th' barn—fifty cents. Dollar if yer want t' grain yer horses."

"Thank you," said Doc, who had been unhappily considering another night under the stars. "I'll take you up on that offer."

"Yer can have supper fer another fifty cents," the farmer added, growing bolder. "We've et, but my woman'll het it up fer you while yer takin' care of yer horses."

Doc nodded again and rode to the barn. Ten minutes later he returned to the house, where the farmer's work-worn wife dished him up a tin plate of beans and salt pork and then poured him coffee that had been boiling all day on the back of the stove. It was black as sin, laced with chicory or some other herb, and Doc almost choked when he took his first, tentative, sip.

"Ma'am, would you have a tin of milk to thin this a mite?" he asked hopefully. She shook her head and retreated to the next room, where he could hear the boys giggling. Doc sighed and dug into the beans, thinking how Raider would bust his gut laughing over what he had paid for this meal.

The corn bread was good, however; and when he finished, pushing the plate aside, he rolled a cheroot between his fingers, sniffing it appreciatively before striking a match on the underside of the table. He kept turning the cigar until it was burning evenly, and then he drew several satisfying puffs. Then he turned and stabbed a finger toward the oldest of the boys, hiding at the crack of the door to the next room.

"You, son—I won't bite. Come on out."

"Lysander!" That was his mother. Her voice was brittle with fear for her son. But the boy was made of sterner stuff. He opened the door, slipped through, and then stood with his back against it, staring at Doc.

"You hear me tell your pa about the silver that was stolen?"

The boy nodded quickly. "Yessir."

"I figure," said Doc, rolling his cigar to examine the ash, "they must have come this way." He looked up at the boy. "I searched all the roads leading off from the mountain, couldn't find a sign of them. By any chance, do you think you might have seen them?"

"Nosir. Ain't been nobody around here for weeks."

That couldn't be the truth; the pilgrims who discovered the wreckage must have passed by three days before—it was more than three days now since Raider had disappeared.

"No strangers, you mean," said Doc.

"Yessir. No strangers."

"How about people you know?"

"Nosir. Nobody recent, not so's I recollect."

"You around all day? Don't you have to go to school?"

"School's closed for the summer," said the boy, "so's the boys can help at home."

"Um." Doc shook his head. "Well, if you do recall any strangers, anything unusual—say, a stagecoach—why, there might be a dollar in it for you."

"A stagecoach?" The boy stared at Doc as though he were crazy. "Ain't never been no stagecoach around here, sir. Coach don't go up to Coffin but twice a week, and then only by the main road, t'other side of the mountain."

"Well, if you think of anything, just come out to the barn and give me a holler. Good night, Lysander."

"Good night, sir."

Doc left the house, stepping on the remains of his cigar in the dooryard. There was no sign of the farmer or his wife, and the light in the kitchen went out before he reached the barn, leaving the house in darkness. Doc lit a rusty lantern and made his bed in a musty haymow, turning the light down before settling himself in for the night.

He crossed his arms behind his head, staring into the darkness. The barn stank of old manure, old horse piss, old hay, but it was better than sleeping on the ground. Marginally better. He wondered where Raider was sleeping.

Lysander was lying. Probably his father, too. When Doc had asked about the stagecoach, the boy's eyes had gone as big as saucers for the space of a single blink. The boy had seen the stagecoach, probably knew where it was. The problem was how to get the information out of him when his father was nearby with that damn shotgun.

Maybe an answer would come to him while he slept. Doc yawned, cracking a jaw, and rolled over, digging himself a hollow in the hay for his hips and his shoulders. But he didn't sleep for a long time, despite a continuing series of yawns and a true desire to forget his worries, at least for the night.

Doc woke to a massive sneeze as the ammonia smell of the barn got to him. The sky in the east was just beginning to show a faint tinge of light when he went to the door, yawning and stretching the kinks from his body. The house was dark; he studied it a moment, wondering which of the rooms belonged to the boys, and how he might get Lysander to tell the truth. With Raider along, between the two of them they'd soon uncover it . . .

Damn you, Raider! he thought.

There seemed little point in pressing the farmer or his boys. Doc yawned again and crossed to the pump in the yard to splash water on his face. Then he saddled the horses, mounted, and rode out. Breakfast might be available, but after last night's supper, he wasn't going to risk any more money on his unwilling host.

As Doc headed back into the mountains, his thought was that the last two days had been wasted, riding hell-for-leather after his partner. He should have delayed long enough to put together a proper posse, men who might know these trails. Maybe he could've found someone who knew the ranchers.

The sun was up when he stopped to fix himself breakfast from his saddlebags, and it was already hot. It was fixing to be the hottest day yet, and he rinsed out his canteen in a mountain brook, filling it with fresh water. He made good time climbing the road; it was only a little after nine when he reached Graveyard Gap again. He stopped to give it a final look-over, hoping against hope that he had missed something two days before.

The evidence of the dozen men who had waited in ambush was still clear after four days, as were the tracks where the stage had waited in the trees. But they petered out on the road itself, lost in the welter of other tracks laid down since spring had come and the road had opened again.

Leaving the horses to graze in the meadow, Doc walked the short distance down to the slope where the wagon had gone over and stood there studying the canyon below, as though waiting for the mountains to tell him what had happened. At last, he scrambled down the slope—and stopped when he spotted a glint of metal to his right. He moved that way cautiously, picking his way through the loose shale that threatened to slide at any step.

A gun was half-buried beneath the shale—Raider's Remington. Doc cursed softly as he dug it out and released the cylinder. All of the cartridges had been fired.

It was a sure thing that wherever Raider had gone, it had not been willingly. Not without his gun.

Doc slipped the gun into his belt and resumed his downward progress. He could see where a number of men had scrambled across the slope, and he guessed that they had been retrieving the silver. Only one set of tracks seemed to go down into the canyon bottom. The others stopped a hundred and fifty feet higher. Greedy bastards must have wanted every last ingot of the silver.

He slipped and scrabbled, clawing at the loose shale, until at last it gave way and he slid the last hundred feet on the seat of his pants. Doc cursed again as he banged his elbow and a sharp stone scraped along the inside of his thigh, nearly smashing his testicles. He sat up, rubbing the elbow, while dust settled on his clothes. At last he stood and knocked his derby hat against his leg to shake off the worst of the dust.

The bottom of the canyon showed signs of heavy traffic, mule and horse tracks. Much of it was recent, for a pile of dung was alive with flies and ants, although it had stopped steaming. There were half a dozen of the biscuits, but Doc wasn't tracker enough to be sure which way the animal had been headed. He flipped a mental coin and turned south.

A few minutes later the smell of wood-smoke drew him into a side canyon. Approaching cautiously, slipping from tree to tree, he drew the Diamondback. A moment later he spotted the cabin.

The yard was empty, although smoke curled from the length of stovepipe that served as chimney. Doc started to move closer—

"Hold it right there, mister!"

Doc stiffened as a clear, young voice barked the order. For a moment, he thought it was Lysander; but that was ridiculous. He turned slowly so as not to spook whoever had the drop on him.

"Drop your guns."

He tossed the Diamondback onto a mossy stretch and then gingerly drew Raider's empty Remington from his belt and threw that after the Colt. Only then did his captor step from cover—and Doc's jaw dropped.

"A girl!"

"You got eyes," said Amity sarcastically.

"Look here, young lady, you have the wrong idea. I mean you no harm—I'm looking for a friend. Permit me to introduce myself. I am Dr. Weatherbee, itinerant apothecary, seller of nostrums, health secrets and restorers of every kind."

"Bullshit!" said the girl. "Peddlers don't come sneakin' up on a cabin with a gun in their hand. Peddlers don't come down in these canyons at all."

"I assure you, dear child, I am what I say. Perhaps you've seen my friend?"

He described Raider while Amity studied him, the barrel of the Henry held unwavering on his belly. An itch along his spine was nearly driving him crazy—and when she spoke again, Doc jumped.

"Git in th' cabin."

Doc took one step backward and then turned and moved sideways toward the cabin door. Amity followed him, the Henry held steady, and once inside, she kicked the door shut behind them. The cabin was lost in gloom.

"There seems to have been some mistake," said Doc, quickly glancing about the cabin. There wasn't much in the way of furnishings: a rude bed, a ruder table, a single chair, a stove.

"You talk too much, fancy britches," said Amity. And then she said something that made Doc stare at her in horror and amazement.

"Take off yer clothes."

"My dear child—!"

"Shut up, mister!" The Henry moved up until the massive barrel pointed straight at Doc's heart. "You heard me—git outa them duds 'fore I blow your balls off!"

This couldn't be happening! But the Henry was real, and there was steel in the girl's unwavering gaze. Shaking with anger, Doc began to do as she said.

CHAPTER NINE

Doc knew he had walked right into it this time. A girl! She looked to be no more than a child, but the way she held the Henry showed that she knew how to use it.

He felt his insides go sour as he took off his hat and then his jacket, slowly, laying them across the table. He knew he should have waited, spied out the land. Patience was one of the major tools of a Pinkerton operative, and one of the prime causes of arguments between Raider and himself. Raider was always jumping in nose first without looking, trusting to his fists and his guns.

More than once, Doc had been forced to drag his partner out of a tight place; right now, however, Doc seemed to be the one who had forgotten everything in the Pinkerton manual. He felt as though this assignment had been cursed from the beginning. Maybe Raider had been right—they should never have gone near the Denver office. Look what it had brought them.

The girl smiled as Doc bent to pull off his boots, her tongue darting across pert lips. She wasn't bad-looking, and she was enjoying herself as he straightened and started to unbutton his shirt. Doc knew that women in these lonely outposts could be mighty frustrated. This wasn't the first time one had been eager to spread her legs for him, although the situation would have suited Raider better. Doc prided himself on being particular in his choice of bed partners, unlike his partner.

Now the girl shifted the Henry into the crook of one arm and started to undo the buttons of her own shirt. Her intentions were unmistakable. He saw the rise of her breasts against the shirt, saw her eyes drop to his crotch as she checked for visible evidence of arousal. He slipped his suspenders down from his shoulder and shrugged out of his shirt as though surrendering to the inevitable. His hands caught his buckle—

—and Doc moved, jumping before Amity realized what he had in mind. He came up low, under the Henry, and knocked the barrel aside. Before the girl could recover, Doc wrenched the rifle from her hands and followed through, hitting her hard.

"You bastard!"

Amity cried out in sudden anger as Doc hooked his foot between her legs and kicked. She went down hard, the breath knocked from her lungs for a moment. Before she could twist free, he landed on top, his knees pinning her arms to the rough floor.

"Damn you!" Amity tried to claw at Doc's legs, and he brought the barrel of the rifle to the hollow of her throat.

"Be still!" he warned. "Behave yourself, girl, or by God, I'll—"

He didn't need to finish his statement. The girl arched and then fell limp, staring up the length of the barrel at Doc's anger-suffused face. And then she shocked him anew; she laughed.

"You think it's funny?" cried Doc, feeling a sudden rush of shame and embarrassment. Suddenly he felt like a bully for using his strength against her.

"That gun ain't loaded," she said, and then she added, "I been expectin' you."

Doc's back straightened, and he stared suspiciously at the girl and then at the rifle. Half a minute passed before he broke the breech and saw the empty chamber. She had told the truth.

"Why . . . young woman, I should put you over my knee and paddle your behind until you can't sit down for a week!"

"Don't try it, Doc," she said, the smile flickering

out as fire came into her eyes. "You do an' I promise
you, I'll have yer balls fer breakfast!"

For a moment, their eyes locked; then Doc moved
back and stood watching warily as the girl got up,
rubbing her arms. Her breasts showed through the open
buttons of her shirt, the tail of which had been tugged
from her jeans by the struggle. The jeans themselves
were twisted away, several of the buttons popped. Even
in the gloom of the cabin, Doc thought he caught a
glimpse of soft yellow hair coating her belly. Then he
told himself it was his imagination.

"Who are you?" said Doc. "And what do you mean,
you were expecting me?"

"Your partner said you might come by—said I
should keep my eye out fer a dude in fancy clothes.
Not that what yer wearin' is so fancy, 'cept fer the city
hat. But you fit the rest of his description."

"My partner?" asked Doc, still wary.

"John O'Toole."

Doc cursed to himself. If this were another of
Raider's stupid jokes, this time he would kill him!

"Where is O'Toole?" he demanded.

"Shot up kinda bad," said Amity. "Me an' Zach
patched him up best we could, Zach's takin' him up t'
Coffin on th' mule. O'Toole said should you happen
by, t' tell you t' meet him at Gaffney's boardinghouse."

"You better tell me everything," said Doc, sitting on
the chair to pull on his boots. "Start at the beginning—
who is Zach? And just how did John O'Toole come to
be here, in this cabin?"

Amity dusted the seat of her pants, but she didn't
bother to button her shirt, although she hiked up the
jeans. She turned to the stove, poured coffee into a
tin cup, and then offered it to Doc. He accepted, and
she found another cup for herself. The girl then sat on
the bed, drawing up her legs for comfort.

"You know about the ambush?"

"Not enough," said Doc. "Tell me about it."

Amity shrugged and related what Raider had told them. The news that a phony band of Indians had staged the raid surprised Doc slightly, but the information meant little at the moment. He filed it away for future use while she gave him the general outline of what had happened to Raider after the ambush, leaving out only the intimate details that concerned no one but the two involved. Doc could guess those without help.

"His fever broke yesterday," Amity finished. "This mornin', he jest wouldn't wait no longer. He still wasn't up to makin' the ride by himself, so Zach took him up through the canyons—it ain't any shorter, but there ain't no place fer the mule to git up t' the road until yer almost t' Coffin."

"What time did they leave?" asked Doc, buttoning his shirt. He slipped into his jacket, ran a comb through his hair, and put on his hat.

"Fust light," said Amity. "But they ain't gonna be movin' fast, not on Bessie Mae. I figger if'n they make Coffin by four this afternoon, they'll be doin' good. You should catch up to them easy."

"I don't know the canyons," said Doc. "And I left my horses up to the Gap."

"Then you can be waitin' fer them."

Doc sighed, feeling let down now that he knew Raider was alive, if not well. He cursed himself for failing to check out the scene more carefully two days before. That was two full days wasted, when he and Raider could have put their heads together and worked out a further plan of action. Two more days to let the men behind the ambush get away.

He knew Raider would have some choice words to say about his riding headlong into a wasted pursuit, but it couldn't be helped. He opened the door and went out into the yard to retrieve the guns Amity had made him drop. He hoped Raider and the girl would never have a chance to get together again—he'd never live it down if Raider learned that he had been taken with an empty rifle.

Amity followed Doc to the door and stood there with her shirt hanging open to reveal her small but perfectly shaped breasts. The girl's tongue again touched the corner of her mouth as Doc turned back.

"I'm thankful for what you did for my friend, miss— I don't know your name."

"Amity."

"Amity," said Doc. "That's a pretty name."

"You don't have t' be in a hurry," she said. "You got plenty of time to git t' Coffin afore them."

Doc stared as she slipped out of the shirt and undid the top button of the jeans. The heavy fabric dropped like stone to her ankles, and she stood there, posed against the frame of the door. There was no mistaking the thick yellow bush, or the pouting mound behind it. Dressed, Amity had seemed little more than a child. Naked, she might not show a patch to Helena Coffin or her daughters, but she had more than most women could hope for.

Knowing Raider, Doc could understand why his partner had waited this long to return to business.

"Oh, what the hell!" he said, and he went back to the cabin.

CHAPTER TEN

Raider's progress through the canyons was slower than either Amity or Doc could have anticipated. His arm was in a sling, and the fever was not completely driven from his body. He swayed alarmingly on Bessie Mae's bare back, holding on to her rope for dear life with one hand. Cursing, Zach was forced to stop frequently to allow his companion to rest.

"Coulda' been there an' back twicet' over," grumbled the old prospector, helping Raider back onto the mule.

"You've been paid well enough," shot Raider, fed up with the old man's complaints. Not for the first time, he wished Amity had volunteered to be his guide. But the thought of going to Coffin Canyon seemed to terrify the girl.

It was almost dark when Raider finally made out the lights of the mining town on the mountain above. Tailings spilled into the canyon from old workings, and they passed several abandoned shafts. Zach seemed to know his way, however; he led the mule around several treacherous spots that Raider would not have seen.

"I'm leavin' yer up yonder," said the old man suddenly, when they were still a mile or more from the end of the canyon. "Ain't far t' the road," he added, forestalling any possible objection from Raider.

Raider felt sure Zach was reluctant to be seen in Coffin Canyon while he had Coffin silver in his cabin—not that original ownership could be proven. Two days ago, Zach had melted down the original ingots and recast them in his own crude furnace. Undoubtedly he would take them down to Carson City two or three ingots at a time, perhaps mixed in with his own workings.

The prospector halted Bessie Mae in inky blackness beneath an overhang of rock. "This is it, O'Toole," he said. "I reckon you'll be all right now."

Raider slipped off the mule, feeling the weight of his empty gun belt on his hips as he found his land legs. He shifted the sling slightly to ease the ache in his shoulder and then held out his hand.

"Thanks, Zach. For everything."

The old man seemed embarrassed. "Twarn't nothin' any decent body wouldn't have done. Besides, the gal was grateful fer the company." He made a motion. "Go on, straight through there, an' you'll be fine."

With that, Zach was gone, leaving Raider to his own devices. He stared into the darkness of the canyon, hearing the sound of Bessie Mae's hooves; then Zach slapped the mule's flank, trying to hurry her along.

It wasn't until the noise of their progress had died away completely that Raider turned and started along the treacherous canyon, picking his way carefully through the darkness. Several times he was raked by brush that he could not see. Other times, loose rock slipped beneath his boot. More than once, he nearly fell, caught himself awkwardly with his one free hand, and struggled onward.

And then the canyon started to rise and widen. The way became easier, a regular path with firm footing. The granite rock walls were gray in the moonless night. They looked snow-covered, although it was warm enough for Raider to work up a sweat that attracted a buzzing cloud of insects. Several times he slapped at whining mosquitoes, cursing. He could hear the running water that allowed the mosquitoes to breed, and a moment later he splashed through a small creek, and on—

A black figure rose out of the shadows.

Raider stopped suddenly and reached for his missing gun. The other man moved toward him.

"You dumb sonofabitch!" said Doc. "I swear to God, you need a nursemaid to keep you out of trouble."

Raider sighed. "About goddamn time you showed up, Doc. Where the hell you been?"

"Chasing you. I've got horses."

Raider swayed. "I don't think I can . . . ride . . ."

Suddenly he fell forward against Doc. The latter cursed in surprise and started to step backward; then Raider's dead weight carried them both to the ground. Doc could feel the fever flush through his partner's shirt.

"You dumb sonofabitch!" he said softly.

Raider heard murmuring voices. He opened his eyes and smelled disinfectant. He was in bed; a lamp turned low burned on a marble-topped table. His shoulder ached, a low throbbing that seemed to echo the beat of his heart. He tried to shift to a more comfortable position and moaned as the ache turned to a stab of fire.

"Mr. O'Toole!" A middle-aged woman rushed through the door, which had been ajar. "Don't try to move—I'll get someone to help you."

She rushed out as quickly while Raider breathed shallow breaths; a moment later, Doc and Junius Coffin came into the room. The former came to look at the dressing while Coffin stood at the foot of the bed.

"Where am I?" asked Raider.

"In my house," said Coffin. "Do you feel up to talking?"

"For God's sake, give him a chance!" said Doc. "Take it easy, Rade—you've lost a lot of blood."

"How long have I been here—how long since the shipment was taken?"

"You've been here since yesterday," said Doc. "Five days since you were ambushed."

"Five days, and not a sign of the silver," said Junius Coffin bitterly.

"I want a drink," said Raider. Doc picked up a water pitcher. "Whisky, damn it!"

Doc seemed doubtful, but after looking at Junius, he left, returning a few minutes later with a decanter of brandy and three glasses. He poured a small amount for Raider and held him up to sip at it; then he poured larger glasses for Coffin and himself.

Raider choked as the brandy burned its way down. Then he sighed, blinking. "What time is it?"

"Just past nine," said Doc.

"Can you tell us anything about the thieves?" demanded Junius impatiently. "Anything at all?"

"They were dressed up as Indians. A dozen of 'em, maybe fourteen or fifteen. We got a few. Not enough."

"You're sure you killed some of them?" said Junius. "They took their wounded and dead with them. You didn't hear any of their conversation?"

"Just some shouting," said Raider. "Nothing clear."

"They were waiting for you, though," said Doc, "There's no mistake about that?"

"No mistake," said Raider. "The bastards were tipped off we were comin'. That means somebody right here in Coffin Canyon got word out that mornin'."

He pinned Junius Coffin with his eyes, and the owner of the Coffin Queen flushed. "That's impossible! No one—*no one*—knew, except for you and me! You roused the guards yourself."

"Somebody talked," said Raider flatly. "They even knew the road, when we didn't decide on that until the last minute. I'm tellin' you, they were ready for us. You have a traitor inside your own company—maybe right inside your family."

"And what does that mean?" said Junius hotly.

Raider shrugged. "You don't get along with your brothers, it's common gossip. The first day I was here, I heard that Jonathan thinks you hold too tight to the purse strings. You don't give him what he thinks is his fair share of the profits. And from what I was told in the saloons, Jasper thinks he should be runnin' the operation."

"Gossip!" spat Junius. "Ungrateful wretches! They draw good wages and spend their idle hours running down the good name of their employers!"

Doc stirred uneasily. "It's something that must be considered," he said. "It wouldn't be the first time troubles came from within the family."

"Well, there'll be no profits to share if these depredations are not stopped!" said Junius. "If we lose many more shipments, we'll have to close down the mine."

Raider and Doc stared at him for a moment. Doc put the question: "Are things that desperate?"

"Close enough to it," said Junius unhappily, pouring himself another brandy. "We can't stand much more."

"Has anyone offered to buy you out?"

"What?" Junius shook his head. "No, no one."

"I still say it's an inside job," said Raider stubbornly. "If not your brothers, it must be somebody close to you. Who stands to take over if you're forced to resign? Jonathan?"

"No, of course not. Under the partnership agreement, Jasper succeeds me."

"And then Jonathan succeeds Jasper?" said Raider.

Junius surprised them with his answer. "No. Jonathan was just a boy when the partnership agreement was drawn up. If neither I nor Jasper can perform our duties, control passes to an executive board drawn from our bankers and our lawyers."

"I want the names of those board members," said Doc. "We'll have to check out all of them."

"But that's preposterous!" protested Junius. "Some of the most respected men in San Francisco are on that board. Some of the wealthiest."

"Even rich men find themselves needing money,"

said Doc. "Some aren't too particular how they get it. Just to cover all possibilities, we'll check them out."

"Whoever is behind the raids," said Raider, "must be operating from somewhere in the area. Unless they're locals, live right here in town."

"Impossible!" said Junius. "Everyone in town works for the mine."

"Not quite," said Doc. "You've got storekeepers, saloon owners. But whoever they are, they must have excellent communications. They had only a few hours to round up the gang."

"Locals could pull it off," said Raider, thinking. He absentmindedly shifted position and sucked in a sharp breath; then he let it out carefully and went on, "But they must have someplace to go where they hide the silver. I can't see 'em bringin' it back here."

"It would take an army to scour the mountains for every possible hiding place," said Doc.

Junius shuddered at the thought. Then suddenly he reversed his former position. "Why does it have to be an inside operation?" he asked. "After all, anyone with sense would know that armed guards meant a silver shipment. And there are only three roads out of town a shipment could take. All they had to do was watch and send word ahead."

"How'd they get the stagecoach to Graveyard Gap so fast?" asked Raider.

"Perhaps they had all three roads covered," suggested Junius, a bit lamely.

"It's possible," conceded Doc. "That would mean a lot bigger gang than we originally thought."

"It does make sense," insisted Junius. "After all, they knew we had to make another shipment soon. It was just a matter of waiting, probably no more than a few days."

"Is anyone missing from the mine, or the town?" asked Raider. "Those fellas I killed came from somewhere."

"Hard to say," said Junius. "We have a lot of drifters who come in, work for a few weeks to put together a stake, and then move on. It couldn't be any of the foremen or supervisors, or Jasper would have said something."

"It could be a combination of insiders and outsiders, then," said Doc. "Certainly they had a contact here. Did you think to check the telegraph office to see if anyone sent messages out that morning?"

"There was nothing—just the message to you, saying the shipment was on its way. And that was in code."

"It was a wild shot," said Doc. "They could have tapped into the line anyplace with their own equipment," he added, thinking of his own key hidden in the bottom of the wagon.

"Which puts us right back where we started," said Raider.

"What about Zachariah Gilchrist?" said Junius, scowling. "That old scoundrel has been stealing silver for years, tapping into the Queen's old shafts. I wouldn't be at all surprised if he were involved."

"Then why did he save my ass?" asked Raider. "I think you're all wet on that score. Zach's okay."

For a moment, the three men were silent, brooding, lost in their own thoughts. Then Doc saw that Raider had drifted into sleep again.

"There's nothing more we can do tonight," he said quietly, leading Junius out of the room. "Get me that list of names, and in the morning I'll wire San Francisco to start checking them out."

"What will you be doing in the meanwhile?" asked Junius sourly.

Doc shrugged. "It'll be several days, maybe a week, before Raider can travel. For a while, I'll stick to my cover as a traveling medicine man, see if I can scout anything out of the townsfolk. I made sure nobody saw me bring Raider here, and I assume you can keep your wife and servants from talking. We better avoid contact—drop any messages in the wagon. I'll come back at midnight tomorrow, so make sure the back door is unlocked."

Junius sighed. "I must tell you, my patience—our patience—is limited. Nor can the Queen afford to continue paying good money to Pinkerton's without some concrete results. Jasper wants me to put you on a timetable."

"Mr. Coffin, Pinkerton's does not and cannot guarantee results," said Doc, heating up. "But you know our rate of crimes solved is far greater than that of any municipal police force in this country. If necessary, the agency has been known to spend years on a case after the original client withdraws—particularly should one of our agents be killed. If anyone can track down the person or persons behind your silver thefts, it will be Pinkerton's."

"Nonetheless," said Junius, "I am not completely free in this matter. I can give you two weeks, no more. If you haven't brought this case to a satisfactory conclusion, then we'll have to consider alternatives."

Fuming, Doc left the house without saying good night. He hated the pressure of a deadline, although in honesty, he could understand Junius' feelings. Leaving by the back door, he waited to be sure the street was empty before coming out of cover.

The town was quiet, two of the four saloons shut down for lack of business; payday was two days away. But there was activity in the shafts that honeycombed the mountain, deep beneath his feet. Doc imagined the pulsing life that existed there, a great beating heart pumping the silver from its ancient caches into the world of men.

He headed for the hotel and another unsatisfactory night in the sprung bed, thinking that tomorrow he would move into Raider's boardinghouse. Bed and board were both rumored to be excellent, and it would be convenient to share a roof with his partner, once

Raider was able to leave Junius' house—if they were to remain on the job long enough to make a difference.

As he passed the yard of the Coffin Queen, he could smell the stink of the mine stables. Somewhere in the distance, a dog yipped for nearly a minute until a hoarse voice shouted at it to be still. CeeCee Coffin's big house was ablaze with lights. Doc heard voices as he rounded the corner and saw a carriage standing in the drive. The girls, Moravia and Zelzah, were climbing the steps to the porch while an Indian servant struggled with trunks and luggage. A diminutive figure that must have been CeeCee himself was helping Madame Helena to alight. There was no mistaking that buxom figure or towering headdress.

Doc quickened his pace, intending to hurry by, but he was too late; she had spotted him. Madame Helena stared in pleased surprise and then called his name.

"Dr. Weatherbee! What a stroke of fortune!"

CHAPTER ELEVEN

Doc's mind raced as he stopped dead in his tracks and then reluctantly turned toward Madame Helena. He couldn't remember what he had told her in Virginia City, whether he had given her the story about representing a foreign mining syndicate. If so, how would he explain being in Coffin Canyon with his wagon?"

"Good evening, Doctor!". Madame Helena said warmly. "It is such a pleasure to see you again—I was just telling my husband that he should have such good medical advice as you gave Zelzah. CeeCee is feeling poorly.

Doc forced a sickly smile as he looked at the father of the Coffin brothers. CeeCee wasn't much over five feet tall, a gnome of a man with a thick mane of white hair and matching muttonchops. A vulpine expression was on his florid face, and next to his wife, he seemed no bigger than a boy. He stared at Doc with watery gray eyes that nevertheless seemed briefly sharp and penetrating; but he couldn't focus on any one object for more than a few seconds before his eyes darted elsewhere, like those of a frightened bird.

"Who are you?" asked CeeCee in a high-pitched voice, backing up behind the bulk of his wife. "Who is he, Helena? I know him, don't I?"

"I was unhappily surprised to find that you had left Virginia City so suddenly," said Helena, ignoring CeeCee's plaintive questions. She smiled coyly, showing an improbable dimple. "I was looking forward to further . . . conversations, Doctor."

"Ah, yes." Doc swallowed. "The press of business, madame . . ."

"Well, now that you're here in Coffin Canyon, I won't let you slip away so easily. You must promise that you'll come to dinner tomorrow night."

"If I can," said Doc, "it will be my pleasure."

"No if's!" said Helena, wagging a finger. "I warn you, Doctor, I can be a very determined woman."

There was no mistaking the sexual invitation in her tone and in her eyes. Doc cursed his luck. Maintaining his cover was going to present an additional complication, as was staying out of her embrace.

"I do know you!" said CeeCee suddenly. "You're the grocer's boy—oh, bother!" He waved a hand. "Now, don't tell me, I'll have your name in a minute."

"No, CeeCcc," said Madame Helena. "This is Dr. Weatherbee, not the grocer's boy."

"Weatherbee?" CeeCee shook his head. "I don't know any Weatherbees—unless you're that thimblerigger they strung up in Hangtown back in '51. But of course, you can't be," he added, his confusion growing. "Can you?"

Helena captured her husband's arm. "You must forgive CeeCee, Doctor. He often mistakes people. Dr. Weatherbee is coming for dinner tomorrow, CeeCee—perhaps he can take a look at that leg of yours."

"Why would I let a thimblerigger look at my leg?" demanded CeeCee Coffin. "I swear Helena, sometimes you just don't make sense."

He was loony, just as Zelzah and Moravia had said. Helena turned away with a last smile at Doc. "Until tomorrow evening, Dr. Weatherbee. Seven o'clock, don't forget!"

Doc nodded, nonplused, and watched Madame Helena mount the steps to the porch of the big house. At the last minute, CeeCee turned to look back at Doc. In the light of the carriage lamp beside the door, his eyes seemed filled with hatred. Doc was startled, but before he could confirm his impression, they had disappeared into the house. He wondered if CeeCee knew about his wife's extracurricular activities in Virginia City.

Shaking his head, Doc headed for the hotel. As he settled for the night, his last thought was of the tricks Madame Helena could work on a man. . . .

In the morning, Doc completed his move to Gaffney's boardinghouse. He wasn't surprised when the hotel keeper refused to refund the difference between the daily and the weekly rate, and he didn't bother to argue with the woman over half a dollar. He could imagine the sneer on Raider's face if his partner knew he had let himself be bamboozled, but that was part of the difference between them.

A crowd was coming up the street from the mine when Doc carried his carpetbag into the boardinghouse. A dozen or more men surrounded a flatbed wagon, and when it stopped just outside, he saw that two injured men were in it. One rested on a door that had been taken from its hinges, while the other's arm was wrapped in a temporary sling. Both were bloody. The man with the injured arm could walk, and the other man was lifted out of the wagon and carried into the boardinghouse.

"Easy now!" said an officious man in a vest, bow tie, and bowler hat. "Put him down in the parlor, right there—Mike Fiddler, git them chairs outa the way. Where the hell's the goddamn doctor?"

"He's comin', Horace," said someone else, a messenger who had just run up the steps, out of breath. "He'll be right along."

"Careful with that door!" shouted Horace as the litter bearers nearly dumped their man on the floor. "Assholes!" The injured man moaned with the pain.

"Here now, you men clear out!" Mrs. Gaffney appeared from the back of the house, carrying a steaming pan of water and a dozen towels over her arm. "Go on, now, you're just in the way."

On the fringes of the crowd, Doc fell back with the others as a stout man in graying muttonchops hurried into the house. Carrying a medical bag, he paused to gasp for breath and then went into the parlor. At his direction the sliding doors were closed, shutting out the idle and the curious.

"What happened?" asked Doc.

"Cave-in in number thirty-three," said a miner who stood nearby. All of the workmen were dusty with rock dust, and most of them were red-rimmed about the eyes and streaked with sweat. Several were noticeably rank.

"Side-beam came down," said another. "I don't think Ed Timkins is gonna make it."

Suddenly there was a scream from the parlor, and the men edged nervously toward the door. The scream was followed by a series of groans that gradually died away, and Doc resumed his questioning.

"Are there many accidents?"

"That wa'n't no accident," said another man, the twang of New England in his voice. "Someone pulled that damn beam down!"

"Shut up, Fulton!" said another. "You know better than to run off at the mouth like that."

"I know what I know," said Fulton obstinately. "An' you can't tell me different, Phineas Cassidy." He glanced around. "You fellas can do as yer pleased, but I'm turnin' in my time!"

The sliding door opened far enough to let out Horace, who caught the last of Fulton's words. He advanced on the miners, glaring.

"What the hell do you men think yer doin'? Git back to work 'fore I tell the paymaster t' dock yer wages! There ain't nothin' you can do fer those two fellers, so go on, git!"

The miners left. Horace gave a sour glance at Doc. "Who the hell are you?"

"The name is Weatherbee," said Doc, not bothering to go into his usual spiel. "A guest of the house. Was that man right—that this was no accident?"

"Who the hell says so?" roared Horace. "By God's balls, I hear any sonofabitch spreadin' such vicious rumors an' lies, I'll have his goddamn time card!"

"Horace Meeker!" Mrs. Gaffney appeared in the doorway. "Stop that noise, you hear me? You go on about your business, make your report to the superintendent—go on, now!"

With a red face, Horace tugged his vest into place and popped the cover on a railroad watch; then he started after the men he had chased away. Doc followed him as far as the porch.

"Was anyone else hurt?" he pressed. Horace glanced back.

"I suppose you could say Fred Barnum was hurt," he said sourly. "He's dead."

Frustrated, Doc watched Meeker disappear toward the mine. At the moment, he wanted nothing more than a chance to talk to Raider, discuss this new turn of events. If sabotage was going on, then the case had taken on a new aspect.

But that would have to wait until evening. He also wanted a chance to talk to the three Coffin brothers, but he could do nothing now without running the risk of breaking his cover. The possibility that he could learn more as an outsider made it necessary that he keep pretending to be an itinerant apothecary, at least for a time.

Doc's thoughts were in turmoil as he went up to the second-floor room Mrs. Gaffney had assigned him an hour before. According to her, it was the last room in the house. It was a corner room on the front, with two windows, airy and pleasant, with white daisies on yellow wallpaper. It was furnished with an old rope bed, but the mattress seemed comfortable when he tested it.

Doc unpacked his bag and stowed his clothes in the wardrobe. Then, brushing the dust off his black suit, Doc changed into one more in keeping with his normal image, and twenty minutes later he came downstairs wearing a brown suit with broad yellow pinstripes, a matching paisley waistcoat, a yellow cravat, and bright yellow spats over highly polished shoes. He had put the gray derby aside for one in brown, and carried a gold-headed walking stick.

Mrs. Gaffney came out of the parlor with the water pan and stopped, struck with amazement.

"Why . . . uh . . . good morning, Doctor," she stammered.

"Good morning, ma'am," Doc said politely. "How are the workmen?"

"Timkins punctured a lung," said the doctor sourly, appearing behind her. He wiped his florid brow with a none-too-clean kerchief. "Mattie, did you send the girl for some men to carry him upstairs?"

"They'll be along directly," said the housekeeper, and then she vanished toward the back of the house with her burden of soiled towels and dirty water. The doctor eyed Doc with suspicion.

"Did I hear Mattie call you Doctor?"

"Purely an honorific title," said Doc smoothly. "Permit me to introduce myself—Dr. Weatherbee, apothecary and seller of nostrums, remedies, restorers."

"Snake-oil peddler, eh?" said the other, smiling.

"I like to feel that I bring medical services to those who aren't blessed with a practicing physician," said Doc, refusing to be baited. "I offer primarily homeopathic medicines, although I try to stock the most popular patent remedies as well."

"Just so long as you ain't got the notion of settin' up a practice here," said the other. "In fact, I think it might be a good idea if you was to think about movin' on. The marshal don't take kindly to snake-oil men."

Before Doc could respond to the scarcely veiled

warning, Mrs. Gaffney's serving girl appeared with three men, obviously dredged from the nearest saloon. The doctor directed them into the parlor, ordering them about officiously as they picked up the improvised stretcher. Mrs. Gaffney reappeared to give them directions.

"Mr. Timkins' room is the last one on the left," she said. "Oh, be careful—you almost knocked down the railing! Be careful!"

The other injured man sat in a chair. Doc moved to take one corner of the door and was thanked by the man at the rear. They maneuvered up the narrow staircase and at last got the unfortunate Timkins into his room and into his bed. Two of them got him out of his clothes, Timkins unable to help. The doctor had given him a powerful sleeping draught to ease his pain. As the men left, the serving girl appeared again to sit with him while Timkins snored with bubbling breath.

Doc lingered a moment longer and then went downstairs as the other injured man came out of the parlor, testing his broken arm. He had a large sticking plaster on his forehead and walked gingerly. He glanced up the stairs, shaking his head.

"Poor bastard. He ain't got a chance."

"That will be two," said Doc gravely. "How many others were in the shaft when it collapsed?"

"Just the three of us," said the miner. "We was gettin' ready to close it down. At least Fred caught it quick—the beam crushed his skull. I guess I was the lucky one."

"Do you think it was an accident?"

"Now just what the hell does that mean, mister?"

"That's what some of the others were saying."

"Bullshit! I've worked in silver an' gold mines from Montana to Cripple Creek to the Mother Lode. They're all the same, the owners—too damn tight-fisted to spend money to save lives. All they care about is the silver and the gold, not about the men who dig it out of the ground."

"Then you think it was an accident?" pressed Doc.

"Hell, I don't know—anything's possible. I'll be more careful the next time I go down, though, you can bet your bottom dollar on that."

"What will you do now?" asked Doc, following the man out of the boarding house.

"This goddamn minute? Mister, I'm goin' down to the Silver Bucket and get as drunk as three dollars will get me. Then I'll go home and sleep it off. By the time I wake up, mebbe I'll have figgered out a way to keep food on the table for my wife and kids while this busted wing heals up."

"I'd be honored to buy you your first drink."

"Then come along, 'cause I'm buildin' one powerful thirst. And I don't care whose money I drink on."

CHAPTER TWELVE

Doc spent the next several hours in the saloons, where he soon learned that the Coffins were as unpopular in their own town as in Virginia City. Times were good, but relations with their work force were uneasy. He heard stories about strike-breakers called in three years before, when a militant faction had tried to start a union.

"What happened?" he asked. Doc was at a table with three men, all of whom eyed his fancy suit with suspicion. Then one, the drunkest, shrugged.

"The organizers were thrown into jail, the rest run out of town," he said sourly. "Broken heads, bashed ribs, whatever was wrong—nobody gave a shit, tried to patch 'em up. Marshal give 'em a swift kick in the ass to hurry 'em along."

"Goddamn Pinkertons!" said another.

Doc said nothing to defend the agency. Pinkerton had tried to avoid labor troubles, at least since the days of the Molly Maguires in the coal fields of Pennsylvania. Still, it would be many years before all the bitterness died down.

"Ain't all of 'em gone," said another man. "I figger there was four, five, awful convenient rock slides right about that time. Some of them fellers is still there beneath 'em."

"What about the accident this morning?" pressed Doc. "Do you think it was an accident?"

The three men said nothing. One raised a shoulder and let it drop, and another made rings on the table top with his glass. The conversation seemed to have died, and so Doc moved on.

Stopping to light a cheroot as he left the saloon, he saw a rig turn out of CeeCee's house. Madame Helena was the only passenger. She didn't see Doc, and the rig drove out of town. He remembered Zelzah's comment in Virginia City about her mother's afternoon 'rides.'

The girls didn't seem to have much love or respect for their mother, and Doc wondered if Madame Helena were indeed on her way to meet a lover. He briefly considered following her, but she was gone from sight before he could head for the stable.

Doc's own presence in town was questioned more than once by the naturally suspicious locals, even when he stood several rounds in each saloon. But they seemed to buy his story about being an itinerant apothecary, and more than one of the miners evinced interest in his stock. Doc tried to put them off.

"I have to check in with the town marshal first," he said, recalling the doctor's remarks. "Get a proper license, gentlemen. I'd not want to run afoul of the local law."

One grizzled miner hooted, nearly upsetting his neighbor's glass as he pounded on the bar. "Seth Morgan ain't been sober enough to write up a license since the Queen's wagons started bein' jumped."

"Hell," said another, "I ain't never seen Seth sober."

Doc filed the crack with other miscellaneous bits picked up that morning. He had been apprised of Marshal Morgan's shortcomings as a lawman by a bitter Junius Coffin, but the position was elective and nothing could be done until the next election for local offices, in August. Nevertheless, he stopped in at the marshal's office, where he found Morgan suffering a hangover.

"Who the hell are you?" growled the aging, sagging-gutted lawman, spitting shreds of a cigar in the general direction of the potbellied stove. He was unwashed, the office unswept. Backing off, Doc caught the stink of fouled bedding in the two cells behind the office.

"The name is Weatherbee," said Doc, going into his spiel. Seth Morgan heard him out, grunted something about two dollars, and scrawled on a blank license form. As Doc hurried out, he realized that he had been breathing through his mouth. He also knew that that particular two dollars would never see its way into the town treasury.

Yet Seth Morgan had once been a good lawman, with a decent reputation built in the cow towns of Kansas. He had been in Coffin Canyon for seven years, and during that time he must have been competent to handle Saturday-night drunks and rampaging cowboys. He had been reelected, with Coffin support and without competition, each year.

Doc had gone to the marshal with the idea of enlisting his aid, although at their first meeting, Junius had warned him such a move would be a waste of time. Perhaps it had been too long since Morgan had seen real trouble.

The afternoon passed, and too soon, it was time to face up to supper, and Madame Helena. It was an experience Doc would cheerfully have foregone.

"Dr. Weatherbee!" Madame Helena seemed her most giggly self, answering the door in person and ushering Doc into the front parlor. "We're so glad you could join us—aren't we, CeeCee?"

CeeCee was rocking rapidly in an armless rocker. He looked up at Doc's entrance and grunted; twenty minutes later, Helena had to take him by the arm to lead him into the dining room.

There, the three women competed with one another to see who could pass the most suggestive comments over the head of the unfortunate master of the house, while CeeCee talked to himself in a rapid monotone and built gravy islands with his mashed potatoes, ignoring the badinage of his new family.

"Will you be in Coffin Canyon long, Doctor?" asked Madame Helena, batting her eyes.

"Not very long," he said, drawing back his foot while Moravia smothered a giggle. She had just rubbed the inside of his thigh with her stockinged toe! Doc shot her a glare, but he dared not say anything. Zelzah, next to him, suddenly dropped her napkin and bent over toward him, placing her hand on his leg for support. As the girl straightened, she made a grab for his cock that barely missed.

"What a pity," murmured Madame Helena, her eyes shooting poisoned darts at her daughters. "I had so hoped we would have your company for a while, Doctor. It does get so lonely in a town where there are no equals . . ."

Her voice trailed off with a languid sigh as CeeCee suddenly jumped up and rushed out of the dining room. At the same time Madame Helena rose, tinkling her little silver bell. The Irish maid appeared from the kitchen.

"We'll have coffee in the parlor, Maureen."

"Yes'm." The girl bobbed and disappeared, while Moravia and Zelzah rushed to see who could grab Doc's arm first. Zelzah won, being on the same side of the table, but Moravia refused to relinquish her own grip. Together they ushered him into the parlor again. There was no sign of CeeCee.

"Loony as a jackrabbit with a cactus spine up his tail," said Zelzah, languidly waving a Chinese fan as the girls settled themselves on either side of Doc. "My, isn't it a warm evening, Dr. Weatherbee?"

Doc was sweating, but not from the warmth. Zelzah managed to rest one hand on his shoulder, while Moravia's fingers touched his thigh again, the middle one making a circle. Batting her eyes, Zelzah leaned so close that her chin dug into his upper arm.

The appearance of their mother, followed by Maureen with a silver coffee service, brought Doc to his feet in relief. He caught a pout on Zelzah's face as the girls were forced to move apart, and a smile on Moravia's as Madame Helena settled herself on a love seat, smoothing her skirts.

"I've been thinking, Doctor," she said. "This is a tremendously big house—twelve bedrooms, and eight of them empty. It seems so silly for you to stay at the boardinghouse when we have plenty of room."

"Oh, yes!" said Zelzah, growing excited. "Please say yes, Dr. Weatherbee!"

"Yes, do," said Moravia, her voice throaty. "We'd love to have you."

"It's settled," said Madame Helena. "And the girls will tell you that I don't permit arguments. I'll send Chester to the boardinghouse for your bags."

Doc thought fast, but he was outnumbered and outgunned; he could only surrender, his ears burning.

"That's very kind of you. However, I do have some business to take care of this evening, ladies, so I'd best be on my way to do it." He rose, his balls aching with the memory of his last tussle with Madame Helena. "I may be late, so please, don't wait up for me."

As Doc made his escape, he knew that all three of them intended to be awake when he returned. As he left the house, he had a notion they were planning to split him along the spine and dine on him. They reminded him of a picture he had seen in a book once of a man-eating fish . . . barracudas, the three of them.

He turned toward the business district but ducked across the street as soon as he could to make his way down to the next level. There he picked his way behind unlit buildings until he was past the yard of the mine and could circle around to Junius' house without being seen. A lighted lamp had been left in the kitchen. Doc let himself in the back door and slipped up the backstairs to Raider's room.

"Jesus Christ, it's about goddamn time you came!"

said Raider. "Doc, I gotta get out of this crazy house before I go plumb loco myself."

He was sitting up on the edge of the bed, nervously smoking a hand-rolled cigarette. His dressings had been changed. In the wan light of the lamp, Doc thought he seemed pale, and he was sweating, although a breeze stirred the curtains over the open window. A mosquito whined, and Raider swatted at it with a fly swatter. He missed, and Doc slapped the insect against his own cheek.

"Goddamn things are eatin' me alive, Doc. I gotta get out of this goddamn bed!"

"Have you been up today?"

"Just long enough to use the pot. Jesus, that woman watches me like a hawk—in here every two minutes, plumpin' up my pillows. She must have funneled two gallons of goddamn soup down my throat today."

Raider had never taken kindly to mothering. Doc smothered a smile. "Stand up, Rade, and let's see how steady you are on your feet."

Raider threw back the sheet that was his only covering and stood, wearing only the bottoms of his drawers. He took a tentative step and then walked around the bed.

"I'll be okay, Doc. I can make it."

"Well, maybe so. You don't want to rush things."

"I said I'm okay, dammit! Shit!"

Doc surrendered. "All right, the sooner you're back in action, the better. And Junius will be happy to see you out of your sickbed."

"Did you learn anything today?" asked Raider, sitting on the bed again. New perspiration sheened his upper body, but Doc said nothing about the obvious drain on his partner's strength. Instead, he filled Raider in on everything that had happened, from the accident at the mine to Madame Helena's demand that he move into the big house. At that, Raider scowled and tugged at his ear.

"I don't like it, Doc. It isn't a good idea, both of us bein' so close to the family."

"I'm not happy about it myself," said Doc, sighing. "You don't know that woman, Rade."

Raider screwed up his eyes, studying his partner. He had never seen Doc so buffaloed over a skirt, which made him want to see what kind of a hellcat this Madame Helena could be.

"You really think the accident was a phony?" he asked.

"I've got a feeling. Someone is trying to close down the Queen—maybe they want to force the Coffins to sell out, maybe they just want to put them out of business. The robberies were just a warning."

"Anybody in mind, Doc—one of the brothers?"

"Possibly, although it doesn't make sense."

"I vote for Jonathan," said Raider. "Little pissant sonofabitch."

"It may just as well be a rival mine owner, Rade. But speculating isn't doing us a damn bit of good. We need concrete evidence, not guesses."

Footsteps thudded on the stairs, and a moment later the three Coffin brothers appeared. They shared unhappy expressions, and Jonathan was flushed with alcohol.

"I thought I heard you come in, Weatherbee," said Junius. "Have you learned anything?"

"A great deal," said Doc. "I don't know whether it means anything or not."

The brothers looked at one another. They clearly felt awkward standing, but there was only one chair in the room. No one wanted to be the first to grab it, although Jonathan swayed in a circle that soon had Doc blinking dizzily.

Jasper sighed. "Something must be done—too many lives have been lost. And now the trouble has spread to the mine itself."

"You mean the accident this morning?" asked Doc.

"There's been another accident," said Junius heavily. "A misfire at the working head of number thirty-eight. The dynamite was fired before the crew could take cover."

"Anybody killed?" asked Raider.

"No, but it's only by the grace of God," said Jasper. "Several of the men are cut up pretty badly."

"Most of the rest of the shift walked off the job," said Junius. "There's a meeting down at the Silver Bucket—they're talking about staying out."

"Goddamn assholes!" said Jonathan thickly. "Not worth a tinker's damn, the lot of them!"

"This isn't a strike," said Jasper. "The men are worried, and I for one can't blame them. With the guards lost with the shipments, and with what happened today, we've lost nearly twenty men."

"Perhaps we should shut down," said Junius wearily. He had aged in the weeks since Doc and Raider had met him in Denver. "At least until we clear up this matter."

"Shit, that's just what they want us to do!" said Jonathan. "Besides, closing the mine won't solve the problem of the ambushes. We can at least be stockpiling silver for the time we can try another shipment."

"I agree," said Doc. "Closing the mine would be a mistake. Whoever is behind this seems to be getting desperate and desperate men make mistakes. All we have to do is keep the pressure on."

"Seems to me they're more cocksure than desperate," said Raider. "They're so damn sure we can't stop them, they've moved right into the mine."

"Perhaps," said Doc stubbornly. "But we do have something to work with now."

He studied the faces of the three brothers. If one of them was behind the troubles, wanting to hog the Queen for himself, there was nothing to say which it might be.

"You'll have to reassure the miners that something

is being done," he said. "Now that Raider is on his feet,
I suggest we start a patrol through the mine itself—
three or four men you trust, just to circulate and be
seen. They might even stumble on something."

"Are you up to heading the patrol?" asked Junius
sharply, looking at Raider.

"I'm as good as I'll get stayin' in bed."

"All right, we'll try it. But if this doesn't work, we
won't be able to get a man from fifty miles around
who'll be willing to go down into the shaft."

After another minute of useless talk, the brothers
left. Raider just glared at Doc. Once again, he had been
given the shitty end of the stick.

CHAPTER THIRTEEN

Three days later, Raider half-opened one eye and rolled over with a groan, his head throbbing as though the blood vessels in his temples were about to burst. Someone must've been using his skull to drive railroad spikes, and his mouth was full of cotton wool. He dragged his swollen tongue across his teeth, nearly gagging at the terrible taste, and sat up, moving slowly. His left nostril twitched, and his right eyeball felt as though it had been gouged out and carelessly stuffed back into the socket.

Jesus! What the hell had he been drinking last night? He couldn't remember, although there was the blurred recollection of staggering from saloon to saloon, singing with Doc at the top of their voices.

But that couldn't be right. Except for clandestine after-dark meetings, for the past three days he and Doc had been avoiding each other. He opened both eyes at the same time and looked dully around his room in the boardinghouse. A belch erupted, and he caught his throat between thumb and forefinger, holding his breath. The spasm passed, and he swallowed, relieved that he wasn't going to be sick.

"Oh, Christ!" he said aloud, combing his fingers through his hair as he came to his feet and set about the unhappy chore of washing up. Doc should come up with a cure for a hangover, he thought. He'd make his fortune, and they could both quit this goddamn sneaking around.

"Oh, shit!" Raider suddenly remembered something: he had arranged to meet Doc down in the mine at eight this morning. He found his watch on the dresser and popped the cover: past nine-thirty already. Sonofabitch!

In the last two days, Raider had organized a patrol, four men on each of the three shifts. Trusting no one, he had arranged it so that there were always at least two together, should one be in the pay of the other side. Nothing had happened since the first two accidents, and the presence of the patrol had been enough to convince the miners to return to work.

Now, on Sunday morning, when the work force was off for the day, Doc wanted to check out the mine for himself. He still was going out of his way to avoid being seen with Raider, and so they had planned to enter the mine separately.

But Sunday morning had the nasty habit of coming after Saturday night, and Raider had spent the night trying to drink Coffin Canyon's four saloons dry, with only a bit of help from the rest of the town. He made a face as he checked himself in the mirror and decided against shaving. Good liquor couldn't have made him feel this bad. One of those bastardly bartenders had substituted cheap whisky for the best brand Raider had ordered. In his cups, he never accepted less than the best to be had.

Late as he was, Raider took his time about dressing. Doc had waited this long, he could wait a bit longer. He stopped in the kitchen to beg a cup of coffee, but he turned down breakfast. His stomach was still too queasy.

It was a beautiful morning, the air crystal clear. The coffee helped settle his stomach, and his head felt better as he breathed deep. Soon he was stepping briskly along the empty street, almost enjoying his walk. He heard the buzzing of insects, but not a sound of human life. The saloons were closed, the decent folk in the white-painted church at the far end of town, the indecent citizens still sleeping off their hangovers.

The boardinghouse was two streets above the mine. A shortcut led through a vacant lot and down through a gully that wasn't big enough to be called a canyon but still bore the name of Welch's Cut. A stream ran down the Cut, perhaps the same one that ran through the canyon below, where Zach Gilchrist had left him. As Raider scrabbled down the bank of the Cut and started to leap the stream, he heard a clear, tinkling laugh floating down.

He stopped dead in his tracks, looking up the Cut, as the laugh was answered by another. Girls, by God! They were quite a distance above him, but even as he listened, he heard a faint, outraged, "Zelzah!" and knew they were Helena Coffin's daughters.

Doc had been staying at the big house, claiming that there was no easy way out of Madame Helena's clutches. Raider had caught sight of the three women on the street, and he understood Doc's reluctance. Deciding Doc could wait a bit longer, he began to pick his way up the Cut.

Half a mile up, just below the spring that fed the mountain brook, a natural stone basin formed a pool that was protected on three sides by trees and by the mountain itself. As Raider picked his way through the brush, he realized the nearest house was a quarter of a mile below. By a fluke, the breeze had carried the girls' laughter to him in the Cut, but now he saw the two of them standing waist-deep in the pool. Mother-naked.

Raider swallowed, forgetting Doc and forgetting his hangover, as Moravia splashed her sister, bending until her full breasts nearly touched the surface of the pool. The water must have been as cold as Hell's icebox, but the girls were laughing and enjoying themselves. Raider could clearly see Zelzah's bountiful bush through the crystal-clear liquid.

Moravia began to swim, turning on her back, her nipples hard and erect. Three kicks carried her to the bank, and she began to float, toying with her nipples with her fingers while Zelzah ducked farther into the water.

"Lord, I'm horny!" said Zelzah, coming up to stand beside her sister. Her hand rubbed her mound to emphasize her words.

"You'd think Mama would at least give us a chance at him," said Moravia, pouting. "I swear, she wants every cock in the world for herself. Greedy old thing!"

"All *I* know," groaned Zelzah, "is that if I don't get fucked soon, I'll just dry up and blow away!"

Raider was hard. His prick pushed against his buttons, trying to burst out of his pants. He eased the fabric a bit, his face burning with desire, and stepped back, and kicked loose gravel that rattled down into the pool. The girls stood up straight, looking toward his place of concealment.

"Who's there?" said Moravia angrily. "Come out of there right now, whoever you are!"

"It's those boys," said her sister. "You said there wouldn't be anybody around this morning!"

Raider stepped out, turning his hat in his fingers. The hat helped hide his hard-on.

"I'm sorry, ladies," he said. "I didn't meant to spy on you—but I couldn't rightly help myself. Not when I saw two such pretty gals as you."

The girls gasped as they first caught sight of Raider. Zelzah at first tried to cover her breasts, but then she burst into laughter as she realized Raider was as embarrassed as she. She let her hands drop and assumed a seductive pose.

"It's a warm morning," she said. "We decided to cool off a bit."

"You look a little warm yourself," said Moravia, swimming to the bank nearest Raider. "Why don't you come on in and cool off with us?"

Raider studied the sisters for perhaps ten seconds, and then he scaled his hat onto a mossy bank and bent to tug off his boots. Less than a minute later, he was buck naked. He left his drawers tangled inside his pants and his clothes in a jumble and dived into the water. He touched bottom, which was shallow, and came up spluttering between the two girls, shaking the water out of his eyes.

The cold water had an immediate effect on his member, but the girls eyed him with a mixture of curiosity and desire, moving closer.

"Do you have a name?" asked Zelzah, her mouth open to reveal the tip of her tongue as she stared at his cock.

"They call me John O'Toole," he said. "I reckon I know who you are."

"My sister and I were having a discussion," said Moravia, placing a hand on his hip. The water came high on his thighs, just floating his prick. "You see, we have this friend, and Zelzah thinks that a certain . . . part of his anatomy is . . . well . . . unusually large. Now I say it's not so big, it's just that she is inexperienced in such matters."

She glanced up, looked him straight in the eye, and grabbed his cock. Raider sucked in his breath as she fondled him until the stiffness was restored. While it was growing, rising at its usual sharp angle, he reached out to touch her breasts, rubbing his palms over her throbbing nipples. She pulled harder on him, smiling as she closed her eyes to pleasure.

"Let me see!" said Zelzah, trying to push in. "Don't be such a pig, Moravia!"

Raider gasped as the girls grabbed him, fighting over his cock. His knees weakened, and he thought they would buckle. He sank back into the water, floating, while the girls maneuvered him toward the one shallow bank. His shoulders hit rock, and the girls moved up, one on either side, Zelzah putting her arm around his neck.

"Oh, he is big!" she said softly, nuzzling his throat. "So big!"

Suddenly, before Moravia could protest, Zelzah climbed over Raider's hips, holding him tightly in the cool water. For an instant, Moravia's hand was trapped between their bellies, still holding to Raider's cock. She released him reluctantly while Zelzah maneuvered until she was in a position to lower herself onto his throbbing rod.

"Ohhhhh!" She gasped in surprise. "Oh, yes!"

"Christ!" muttered Raider, his shoulder aching from the cool water and from her clutch. "Oh, Jesus, be careful!"

Penetration was difficult, the water washing away Zelzah's natural lubrication. But she worked against Raider, nearly bending his prick double while he gasped again, and at last she managed to take him inside. Moravia knelt beside them, holding Raider's buttocks to keep him on the slope of the bank while Zelzah began her ride.

"Oh, sweet merciful Mother of God!" said Raider with a blissful sigh as Zelzah suddenly bit his neck. And then she came, with a strong shudder that made him arch his back beneath her, thrusting up as she tried to hold him down. He pumped a few more times until his own explosion came, clinging to her while the spasms slowly died.

Moravia watched in renewed jealousy as they rested for a moment, and then she grabbed Zelzah by the hips and tried to pull her away from Raider.

"Come on, it's my turn!"

"Jesus, watch it!" said Raider, sitting up as his still-hard cock was caught and given a sharp sideways twist. "Take it easy!"

"You be quiet, John O'Toole!" said Moravia. "Come on, Zelzah, get out of my way!"

The younger girl slipped away and pulled herself onto the bank, smiling dreamily as she let the sun dry her body. Moravia grabbed Raider's cock, cursing when she saw he was losing his erection.

"Oh, no you don't, John O'Toole!" she said.

Suddenly her warm mouth enveloped his prick completely. Raider shuddered again and tried to draw up his knees as her tongue raked the sensitive surface; then he surrendered to her ministrations. Within a minute, he was as hard as ever, and now Moravia moved up to take the same position as her sister.

"Now!" she said. "Ride me, John O'Toole!"

Raider caught the girl's upper arms and thrust up once, then turned her over onto her back and moved into a more comfortable position between her legs. Moravia gasped and then sighed as he pumped with renewed energy, watching her arch her smooth, white body. He saw that Zelzah was fondling herself, and soon the other girl began to writhe in sympathetic motion, fingers digging into her pussy.

"Oh, yes!" sighed Moravia. "Oh, God, yes!"

Raider swallowed and renewed his furious attack on the girl. To hell with Doc! Let the sonofabitch wait! He had taken shit enough these last few weeks. He rode down into Moravia's voluptuous, warm cavern, forgetting his own aches, forgetting the pleasure Amity had given him. To hell with Pinkerton's! To hell with the Coffins and their goddamn mine! To hell with everybody.

CHAPTER FOURTEEN

While Raider picked his way through Welch's Cut toward his rendezvous with the Riley girls, Doc was leaving the yard of the Coffin Queen, ready to explode with anger at his partner. Where the hell was the big ninny? Fists clenched, he almost stomped into the yard of the big house.

Damn! Half the morning wasted!

Doc thought he had impressed on Raider the importance of this tour of the mine when the two had met outside one of the saloons the night before for a brief exchange of words, Doc begging a light for his cheroot. Unless he gave up his cover, there was no other way for Doc to penetrate the security. He had accomplished almost nothing thus far, but there was nothing to say that he'd be any better off if the miners knew he was a Pinkerton.

Doc wanted desperately to explore the Queen, for an idea had been building for the past two days. The silver mine honeycombed the entire mountain, undercutting the town. There were literally miles of shafts, some of which had been abandoned for many years. And judicious questioning of the Coffin brothers had brought out the fact that there might be other, abandoned, entrances to those old workings.

What better place to hide the stolen silver?

The idea had at first seemed preposterous, but the more Doc considered it, the more he liked it. No one would ever think to look inside the Queen itself.

As yet, Doc knew he had nothing to back up his theory, and he had wanted to wait a bit before breaking it to Raider. But the silver might have been brought back up the mountain, perhaps through a series of canyons such as those used by Zach Gilchrist to return Raider. It would explain why Doc had been unable to find a trace of the silver below Graveyard Gap.

And, too, it would lend credence to the idea that the silver thefts were an inside job. Doc had almost come to believe that one of the brothers must be involved, perhaps in an undisclosed struggle to gain control of the mine. If so, his favorite remained Jonathan, who seemed to be frozen out of the active management of the mine. He had less to lose than either Junius or Jasper, and perhaps everything to gain.

As Doc entered the house, the maid was dusting the front hall. He tried to remember her name as the girl turned to flee.

"Just a minute . . . Maureen, is it?" said Doc in his most fatherly tone of voice. The girl stopped and peered around at him. She seemed beaten down by the unreasonable demands of the three women in the house. She was scarcely more than a child, but her face was already lined from work and woe.

"Is Mrs. Cottin here?"

"No, suh," said the girl. "She went fer a ride, Doctor. She tooked a picnic lunch with her."

"Misses Moravia and Zelzah?"

"Oh, they is out somewheres, too. I don't 'xactly know where, sir."

"Thank you, Maureen."

She did flee, then. Doc was relieved to learn that the girls had absented themselves. He was tired of fighting off the advances of their mother, but at least Madame Helena protected him from her daughters. He felt very much like the mouse trying to outrun the playful cat. As yet, the girls hadn't managed to drag him into their beds, but they showed no sign of abandoning the effort.

Madame Helena had been more successful, which

added to Doc's tension. He hadn't spent a night alone since dragooned into the house. Raider had thought the situation funny, but to Doc, the thought of cuckolding a man under his own roof went down painfully. Perhaps he was remembering his Bible-thumping childhood, but he preferred his women unattached.

However, the present predicament did give him further incentive to wrap up this assignment. Doc could almost hear the explosion of anger that would come from Wagner if Junius did hold them to his timetable, but if it meant escaping the clutches of the Coffin women, this was one case he would be happy to leave unfinished.

Not that some progress hadn't been made, although of a negative sort. Reports had come back from San Francisco on the directors of the Queen, not one of whom was in need of money. Doc had also put in a routine request to have Madame Helena's background investigated, wondering how many of her former husbands she had screwed to death. As yet, there had been no reply.

Still burning with anger at Raider for failing him, Doc glanced into the front parlor—and saw that a drawer of CeeCee's large mahogany desk had been pulled out and overturned on the floor. Papers were scattered over the carpet. That seemed queer, but as he stepped into the room, he saw that other drawers were ajar as well, and that books had been pulled from a glass-fronted bookcase and shoved back in haphazardly. One of the bookcase doors stood open.

Sliding doors separated the front parlor from the back parlor, and the doors were slightly ajar as well. Recalling the fright of the maid, Doc moved quickly to open the doors. Both of the parlors were crowded with heavy dark furniture and given a jungle appearance by rubber plants and ferns and hanging vines. The back parlor held an upright piano that had not been played since Doc had been in the house. But it was also empty.

Doc wondered if he had interrupted someone in the process of searching the desk. But who might it have been? And what did he—or she—expect to find?

He picked up the drawer, putting it back into its slot with difficulty; the wood was slightly warped. Then he bent to pick up the shuffle of papers, and a derringer pistol fell out. Doc stuffed the papers into the drawer and broke the action on the derringer. Dust in the crevices said that it hadn't been cleaned or fired for years.

He started to close the other drawers when he sensed the presence of another. He turned; CeeCee stood in the door, glaring at Doc from beneath his bushy eyebrows.

"You won't find what you're looking for in there!"

As always, Doc was slightly surprised to hear the high-pitched voice coming from the miniature of a robust old man. He started to explain his presence, but CeeCee cut off his words.

"I know what you're after, you and all of them! But you won't find it! Not ever! I made sure of that!"

Doc sighed, weary of the whole blamed Coffin family. There was no point in arguing with this crazy old man. He closed the last drawer and started to leave the parlor, but CeeCee moved into his path and hissed an accusation that made Doc stop dead.

"You're after the silver, aren't you?"

"What?" said Doc, amazed. Had the old man somehow found out his real role? But CeeCee rushed on.

"You're just like the rest of the vultures!" cried the old man, clenching his fists and pumping his arms up and down like pistons on a steam engine. He advanced until he was almost chest to chest with Doc. "Vultures, damn ye! Thought you'd fool me, claimin' to be a doctor! Well, I ain't fooled, mister whoever-the-hell-you-are! Not one bit! You come after my silver, just like those boys—call me crazy and force me to sign over my mine! Well, it won't work—you can tell them that for me! The Queen belongs to me! I found it, it's mine! They can't have it!"

Now CeeCee's head bobbed up and down like a bird's. He backed away and began to pace frantically. Doc studied the old man, wondering if he were really as crazy as he seemed. Or was this only an act? If so, CeeCee was good at it. Perhaps too good.

The old man continued to rant. "You come snoopin' around my house—you think I'm crazy enough to keep the silver here?" He forced a laugh. "Stupid, that's what you are, just like the others! Call me crazy behind my back—don't think I don't hear ever' word they say! Them boys and them hussies, shameless, all of them. I know damn well what's goin' on!"

Hussies? Did he know what Helena was doing? Suddenly Doc felt sorry for this pitiful old man, and he tried a shot in the dark.

"Where is it?" he asked gently.

"What?" CeeCee stopped. "What did you say?"

"Where is the silver?"

He cackled. "You're the crazy one, if you think I'm gonna tell you that! No sirree, just you keep right on lookin', mister. Took me twelve years to find it, I ain't gonna make it any easier for you! And them!"

And then he darted about the room, looking into the corners and through the window, and finally closing the sliding doors to the hall and to the other parlor. Satisfied that they weren't being spied upon, he came back to Doc and jabbed a bony finger into his stomach. His voice dropped to a conspiratorial level.

"I won't let them get away with it, you know," he said slyly. "I know my rights, and I know how to stop them. You tell them, you hear? Make them listen. Tell them I know just how to make them stop!"

"Tell who?" asked Doc patiently.

"Those three connivin' sons of mine, that's who!

That silver belongs to me, ever' last bit of it! Helena, she says so, too. That silver is mine and I ain't gonna let nobody steal it from me!"

He turned then and rushed to the door, but he paused in the act of sliding it open and looked back at Doc.

"We'll get you, damn your hides! You'll all be dead and damned in Hell! We'll kill you all, damn you!"

And with that, he rushed from the parlor.

CHAPTER FIFTEEN

Raider extinguished his bull's-eye lantern as he entered the cage and tugged on the signal rope. Half a mile above, the donkey engine responded, and the machinery began to rattle, the sound heard dimly this far down. The cage jerked once and began to rise rapidly toward the surface. It was swaying a bit, and Raider spread his legs for balance. The kerosene lamp mounted on the ceiling of the cage swayed more wildly.

As the cage neared the surface, the temperature warmed from the ever-steady fifty-four degrees of the working shafts. Winter and summer, it never varied. It wasn't quiet; a working mine was never quiet, with machinery rattling, dynamite blasting into the working head of half a dozen different shafts, and ore carriers bringing their precious burden of shattered rock to the surface where it was dumped into the carts and trundled along railroad tracks first to the crushers and then to the smelters.

Raider was relieved when the cage reached the top of the shaft. He stepped out, unconsciously hurrying his step as he took the short walk to the entrance. He put his lantern on a rough wooden table that held an assortment of torches and stepped into the bright sunlight, blinking for a minute until his eyes adjusted to the sudden change.

Raider would never have admitted the fact to Doc, but he hated the mine, hated closed spaces. He could feel the weight of the mountain pressing down on top of his skull every time he entered the workings. He made his tours of the working levels as brief as possible, unconsciously holding his breath during the ride back up. His lungs ached as he breathed in the surface air, and he nodded to the hardcase guarding the office door.

That one looked through him as though he didn't exist. The reappearance of John O'Toole had not exactly been an occasion for celebration, for Raider was resented as an interloper. None of the guard contingent questioned his absence, although a few acquaintances he had made among the miners had been ready to burst with their curiosity. Junius had released the general story about the latest failure to get a shipment through, and Raider could tell most of the truth about his disappearance.

The hardcases who had been pressed into service as guards resented the fact that an outsider had been placed in charge. Raider had a dozen men working the three shifts in the mine itself, two pairs at a time. And the regular force had been tripled, as well, with four men stationed round the clock by the vault that held the smelted silver. A raid on the mine itself was not expected, but it seemed only the better part of caution to be fully prepared.

Raider would have preferred to bring in Pinkerton men for all of the duties, but Junius and Jasper had both balked at the cost. The choices had been mostly made for him, from the limited supply available. Junius had forced the marshal to deputize the increased force. In a rare moment of sobriety, Seth Morgan had seemed eager to prove himself still a man. But he wasn't strong enough to stand against Junius.

Raider sighed as he left the sunlight and entered the office. It was Monday morning; he and Doc had finally met Sunday afternoon, and it had taken fancy talking to soothe Doc's ire.

"Jesus, Doc, I'm sorry, but I was hung over. Shit, you know what happens to me on Saturday night."

"I know, I know," Doc had sighed. "Goddamn it, you let me down. I waited damn near two hours for you to show up at the mine."

Raider had said nothing. He hadn't been about to tell Doc about his frolic with Madame Helena's daughters, or that afterward he had fallen asleep on the bank of the swimming hole and had slept until the sun was well on its way down. If Doc knew, he'd just get pissed all over again.

"What's the big deal?" he had asked Doc. "What's so damn important that you wanted to see the mine for yourself?"

"How much of the workings have you explored?"

"The working shafts. There're half a dozen, no two on the same level."

"You haven't gone into any of the abandoned tunnels?"

"No. Should I have?"

"I think so. I've got a feeling we've been chasing shadows, Raider, when all along the missing silver has been right beneath our feet."

Raider had studied Doc as though he had gone loco. "In the mine? Come on, Doc! That's damn foolishness."

"Maybe so, but hear me out."

He had given Raider the digest of his thinking. His partner had listened, shaking his head.

"It sounds crazy, Doc."

"We've come up empty checking out sensible ideas. We might as well start checking the crazy ones. I want you to get a map of the workings."

"The maps are locked up in Junius' office. I heard the day superintendent ask Jasper for one the other day. He had to wait for Junius to come to open the safe."

"That's interesting. Junius doesn't trust Jasper with the keys."

"It's a combination lock. I think Jasper has it, but

he don't do nothin' without checking with Junius first. I've been thinking, Doc—Jasper has just as strong a motive as Jonathan, if it's control he wants. Junius treats him like a dumb puppy—scratches him behind his ears when he's good and kicks him when he pees on the floor."

"I think the old man knows something about this, too."

"CeeCee?" Raider had laughed again. "He doesn't even know what day it is, Doc."

"Maybe. Then again, maybe it's all an act." He had described his encounter with CeeCee. "I think he was trying to tell me something, Rade."

"Then why didn't he just come right out with it?"

"Because he's scared."

"Huh. Well, you're in position to know. What do you think they were lookin' for in his desk?"

"I don't know. I looked through the papers, but they were mostly household bills and receipts. Nothing important, but the important item could have been removed."

"Try and make friends with him, Doc."

"It won't be easy. You'll get the map?"

"Probably be a bunch of maps. Yeah, I'll get them, tomorrow. But I still think you're reachin' for the moon."

"Maybe so; maybe not. However, there's no need to tell Junius exactly what you have in mind—just say that you want to get a fix on the whole workings."

"You suspect Junius, too?"

"Hell, I almost suspect you and me. Just play it close to the vest."

Junius was cloistered in his office when Jasper relayed Raider's request for the maps. The oldest Coffin brother came out, perplexed.

"Why do you want the old maps?"

Raider gave Doc's explanation. Junius pinched the bridge of his nose, scowling.

"That hardly seems necessary."

Raider took a step toward the smaller man, swelling like a gamecock about to attack its opponent. He was sick of this job, sick of these people, sick of everything that had happened. He resented the fact that he hadn't been on his feet and able to follow the raiders who had ambushed the silver shipment—he, by God, would have found their trail! Junius backed away in alarm.

"Mr. Coffin, you hired Pinkerton's to do a job. Now, my partner an' I are tryin' to do the job the best way we know how. We've been doin' this kind of work for years, and we've got a pretty good record for solvin' cases."

"Now, take it easy, O'Toole—"

"I don't give a bucket of warm spit whether or not you get your silver back, or even find out who stole it, 'cept that Pinkerton's made it my job to do just that. So, my partner and I are tryin' to recover it for you. The fact that those sonsabitches tried their damnedest gives me a personal stake in this, too, but I could handle that on my own. Now, if you want to hamstring Doc and me in carryin' out our duties, for which you're payin' good money, that's your goddamn business. But don't bitch that you don't like the way I do my job unless you let me do it!"

He ran out of breath and sucked air into his lungs as though winding up for a second blast. And then he turned away in disgust. For Raider, normally short on words, it may have been the longest speech of his life.

"You can't talk to me like that!" said Junius, pushing again now that Raider seemed to be in retreat.

"Bullshit!" Raider spun back, and Junius backpedaled again. "You want to fire me, that's your privilege. Just remember, you called us to help you. Now, do what you damn please!"

Junius surrendered, deflated. "All right," he muttered, "you can have the maps. I still think it's a waste of time."

"You want to be careful going into some of those tunnels," said Jasper as Junius turned back toward his office. "The shoring may have rotted, and it could be dangerous. We can't be responsible for anything that happens."

Raider started to reply when suddenly an uproar broke out in the yard. Junius stopped in the act of spinning the dial on the safe and came back out, and the three of them and two clerks pressed toward the door to see a small crowd of men explode from the mine's entrance.

"What's going on?" demanded Junius, letting out the anger he had been unable to throw at Raider.

There were a dozen men, crowding around two who carried a stretcher. The mood was clearly anger as they shoved one another in their eagerness to be the first to reach the office.

Then Horace Meeker, the day foreman, stepped to the front of the crowd and held up his hands to prevent the miners from pushing their way into the office.

"Set him down right here, boys. Borden, you go git Doc. The rest of you, git back to work!"

But the men showed no inclination to follow his order. Several of them started to shout at the same time, until Meeker used his own lung power to drown them out.

"Goddamn it, shut up! Cassidy, damn you, I said git back to work! There's nothin' more you men can do here."

"What is it?" said Junius, stepping out of the office and glaring at the unruly men. "What's the meaning of this, Meeker?" He didn't ask what had happened to the man on the stretcher.

"Trouble, Mr. Coffin," said Meeker, moving closer

to his employer and dropping his voice several levels as he removed his bowler hat and wiped sweat from his forehead with his shirt sleeve. "There's been another accident."

"I can see that," said Junius, scowling. "What happened this time?"

"It's John Williams—that Welshman who's been mouthin' off, agitatin' the men. I tol' you he was a troublemaker. He's been stirrin' up the men with crazy talk about strikin', Mr. Coffin."

"I told you to fire him!" snapped Junius.

"Yeah, well, I was goin' to. But he didn't come on with the shift this mornin'. The dynamite crew found him about twenty minutes ago, in number thirty-six. We stopped work there two weeks ago—the vein petered out. They was after some charges they left there."

"What happened to him?"

"Rock fell from the roof, near as I can figger. Big one, fifty-pounder or more."

"Is he dead?"

"He was breathin' when we brought him up."

"It was no accident!" shouted one of the miners. "It was murder!"

"Shut up, Schneider!" cried Meeker, spinning around. "Goddammit, you men git back t' work right now, or the whole blamed lot of you is fired!"

"We ain't gonna be kilt like Williams an' Fred Barnum!" cried another. "I say we don't go back!"

Before Meeker or Junius could react to that, the doctor arrived, huffing and puffing. He stopped to catch his breath, fist clenched against his heart; then he knelt beside the stretcher. He felt at the neck for a pulse, peeled back one eyelid, and then stood, dusting off his trousers.

"Too late," he said, blowing his nose into a bandana. "He's dead."

"Shit!" said Meeker. Then he sighed. "I'll take care of it, Mr. Coffin."

Junius said nothing. He looked at Raider, forgetting the miners, who had fallen back and separated into several small clusters of worried men; then he turned and went back into the office. After a minute, Raider followed.

CHAPTER SIXTEEN

Raider wished Doc was present, but he had made up his mind that he would take no more of Junius Coffin's bullshit. He followed the Coffin brothers into the inner office and took a seat, tilting back in his chair while Junius stared. He rolled a cigarette, licked it with his tongue, and, when it was burning evenly, he propped his feet on the corner of the desk.

"Get your feet off my desk!" snarled Junius. "You're going too damn far, O'Toole!"

Raider let the front legs of the chair thump on the floor, fixing Junius with a steely glare. "Who killed John Williams?"

"Why . . ." Junius purpled. "Are you saying we had something to do with his death?"

"That's nonsense!" chimed in Jasper, his voice a squeak. "You heard Meeker—it was an accident! A rock fell from the roof!"

"Bullshit!" said Raider softly. He leaned forward and pointed an accusing finger toward the brothers. "I saw the back of Williams' head. No fifty-pound rock makes a hole the size of a fist. The miners are right—he was killed. Murdered."

"But . . . why?" asked Jasper, in growing confusion. "Are you accusing us of complicity?"

"He is," said a furious Junius. "You're a damn fool, O'Toole—we have nothing to gain by Williams' death. It's going to cause more trouble, not less."

"Williams was agitating the men to strike," pressed Raider stubbornly.

"Yes, and I don't like such talk. No mine owner will
120

stand by and let it happen. But this is just going to stir up the men—and it'll be worse if you go around saying it was murder, not an accident."

"You can't cover it up. I'm not the only one saw the hole in Williams' head. It was made by a pickaxe, or something of the kind."

"A fine mess!" said Jasper bitterly, throwing up his hands. "And where is Jonathan? Have you seen him, Junius? He was supposed to come in and help me this morning, but he never showed up."

"I've trouble enough without trying to keep track of Jonathan." Junius glowered at Raider. "What do you intend to do about this, O'Toole?"

"For the moment, keep my mouth shut and my eyes open—unless I hear something that convinces me you Coffins are behind this whole mess. In that case, I call my partner and we wire a report to the agency recommending withdrawal from the case. What happens then will be up to the manager."

"We're not stealing our own silver!" said Junius.

"I hope you're tellin' the truth." Raider stood. "I'll take those maps. I might as well get on with what I started."

Junius went immediately to the safe and spun the dial. He dug into a stock of rolled maps piled on a bottom shelf. He unrolled several and selected two, each of which was actually half a dozen maps rolled together. Raider opened one, and saw that it was a vertical view, as though the mountain had been sliced away, and an accompanying overhead view. The two views together gave the changes in elevation and direction in the individual shafts.

"Those should give you what you want," said Junius.

Raider nodded. "Remember, we're workin' in your interests, until and unless we find out you're working a confidence racket of some sort. If you're smart, you'll listen to what we say. You call in a doctor to tell you what's wrong, you don't tell him how to examine you."

"Yes, yes," said Junius. "You're right, O'Toole. It's just that everything has been turned upside down."

Junius was interrupted by the appearance of one of the clerks, a timid man who tapped at the closed door and opened it without waiting for an invitation.

"Mr. Coffin? You better come out, sir."

The cause of the clerk's agitation was easy to see as the Coffins and Raider looked toward the yard. Miners were pouring out of the entrance, more arriving every few minutes as twenty at a time were brought up in the cage. Others, on the other shifts, came into the yard from the street. There were already a hundred or more, milling around and casting dark looks at the office and at the main entrance to the mine.

Meeker and the day superintendent, a man named Cannon, came from the shack that covered the entrance, and now other men came down from the crushers and the smelter. The constant roar of machinery throttled down and became a distant rumble as the machinery continued to turn the vast web of belts and pulleys that were now disconnected from the operating equipment. The contingent of supervisors grew as well, until there were half a dozen crowding together into the office. The Coffins gave way and let them in.

"What is it now?" demanded Junius, heating up again. "Why aren't those men working?"

"I'm sorry, Mr. Coffin," said Cannon soberly. "They say they're walking out, the whole day crew. They . . . ah . . . say they won't go back until the . . . ah . . . murders . . . are solved."

"Damn them!" cried Junius. His was the outrage of a man used to instant obedience from the men who worked for the wages he decided were fair and just, no matter what the personal opinions of those men on the subject. For a minute, Raider thought Junius was going to explode.

Then the air ran out of him, as it had before, and suddenly Junius seemed an old man. He conferred with

Jasper and then with his supervisors, and at last he stepped out of the office. The milling men were talking in subdued voices, and within a minute all had fallen silent.

"Men," said Junius, his voice near cracking, "I understand how you feel. My brother and I agree that the mine should be shut down, at least for a few days, until we get to the bottom of this matter."

He turned then and gave Raider a sour glance. "We've called in outside assistance; detectives, but until they get here, we're relying on you men to help us." No mention of the fact that Doc and Raider were those detectives. "For the moment, we'll be posting an increased guard force, so anyone who is interested, report to John O'Toole. And remember, if you think you know anything at all that might be helpful in solving these unfortunate incidents, don't be afraid to come to one of your supervisors, or to either of my brothers or myself. You can do it in secret, if you want, because I promise you you'll be protected."

With that, Junius went inside, followed by the supervisors. The men continued to mill around for a few minutes, and then Phineas Cassidy climbed to the back of a wagon and shouted for attention. But he spoke without great passion.

"Go on home, boys. Don't make trouble, don't do anything to give the guards an excuse to raise hell. Let the spokesmen you elected do any speakin' for you. But like the big boss said, if any of you know somethin', fer Christ's sake, tell it to somebody. Remember, our jobs are on the line."

A few words were passed, and then several of the foremen came out of the office and picked out the men who tended the driving machinery, sending them to shut down and secure the crushers and the smelter. Only the donkey engine that operated the cage in the mine itself would be kept running. Some of the others drifted out of the yard, returning to whatever they had been about, while a few more came over to Raider, offering their services as guards. He summoned a clerk from the office and signed up a dozen, and then he indicated that he had enough.

The four men who had been on patrol in the mine came up with the last of the exodus, and now Raider posted them, two at the entrance and two more joining the hardcase already guarding the office. He joined the superintendent of the smelter and posted more of the men at the machinery, in case someone should have sabotage in mind.

By the time he had finished making his new arrangements, the miners had left the yard, most of them heading toward the saloons. Raider thought of contacting Doc to bring him up to date, but by now he probably had already heard. Instead, he stepped back into the office and retrieved the maps he had set aside for the moment; then he headed toward the entrance. Strike or not, Doc would still expect him to explore those abandoned workings. With the working shafts empty, there was no time like the present.

CHAPTER SEVENTEEN

After two hours spent climbing over rock falls and picking a careful way around rotting timber, Raider was covered from head to foot with dirt and debris. The heart of the mountain seemed deathly quiet now that the working equipment had been shut down. His skin was clammy, but his face was streaked with sweat-runnels from the tight pressure of his hat band under his chin.

Aching, Raider paused to rub his fist against the small of his back. He had thoroughly checked three of the abandoned shafts, more than once having to take to his hands and knees for short distances. Now, according to the map of the works, a fourth tunnel branched off here and seemed on paper to run all the way to the surface. That was what Raider assumed was meant by "vent" in tiny, crabbed handwriting.

He unrolled the section schematic and brought the bull's-eye lantern close to the paper, retracing his path through the sets of double lines. The rest of the maps had been left back at the cage. The route sketched by the mine's architect seemed clear, although the man himself had moved on several years before. More recently, Cannon, the day super, had also served as architect.

Cursing Doc for the dozenth time this afternoon, Raider rerolled the map and positioned the lantern to shine on the pile of lumber. Doc's idea that the silver had been smuggled back into the mine was plain foolishness. Considering the troubles he had already run into, the roof of the next shaft had most likely collapsed. This whole blamed notion was a waste of time and effort.

Even as he grumbled, however, Raider knew he was going to move that pile. He wanted to rub Doc's nose in this foolishness. He tested his shoulder, which gave off a warning twinge, and sat on the edge of the pile, thinking longingly about a cigarette. The air down here was stagnant, however, and he suppressed the desire. He placed one hand on the board—

Something crawled across his hand.

Raider yipped and glanced down to see a black bug. Cursing out loud, he jumped to his feet and shook the thing away. Raider hated bugs and crawling things. He beat at the seat of his pants to dislodge anything else that might have climbed aboard, and then he grabbed the lantern and brought it to shine on the board. The pile was alive with termites and slugs.

Gagging, Raider backed away, turning the light on his clothes to make sure he had rid himself of the disgusting things. He stumbled on a rough place in the floor, and the light nearly went out. He grabbed it, burning his hand on the hot tin, and cursed again. Then he saw that some of the bugs were in the dirt covering the floor and did several shuffling steps through them, after which he beat a hasty retreat down the shaft.

Goddamn Doc's worthless hide!

He didn't stop until he was halfway back to the first shaft he had explored; and then Raider remembered the map. His terror had subsided, the fear of bugs crawling inside his clothes diminished and he stopped and thought about going back.

"The hell with it!" he said firmly. "Doc wants the goddamn map, let him go get it!"

Holding the lantern high each time he bent beneath a crossbeam to make sure there were no spiders lurking in the shadows, Raider covered another hundred yards before he stopped again. Shit!

It was the log. The decay was what might be expected of wood buried in the ground for years. So why was the bug side turned up?

"Horseshit!" said Raider. Uttering a weary sigh, he turned back. It was almost ten minutes before he reached the pile again; he had been moving fast during the first few minutes of flight, but now reluctance dragged his heels.

He shone light over the pile, examining the whole structure carefully. Some of the bugs scurried from the light. Despite the apparent disuse of these tunnels, the stack had been shifted sometime in the very recent past. But why?

There was probably an innocent explanation, but Raider knew he couldn't leave without checking it out. The nest of termites had settled back again. Wishing he had his gloves, he found a short board and stirred the bugs into flight. Then he grabbed the end of the log and pulled it away. Half the pile came with it. The underside of the log was clean, as were the boards beneath.

Hanging the lantern to give the most light possible, Raider began to attack the stack. There wasn't as much lumber as he had first thought, but that had been carefully positioned to hide the branching tunnel completely. Someone without a map and lacking knowledge of this old section would not have known it was there.

When he had an opening large enough to accept his body, he brought the lantern and poked it through the hole he had made. There was the now-familiar smell of must in the damp air, and somewhere, the drip of water. The tunnel looked as though it hadn't been used for years.

Then he lowered the lantern and saw drag marks in the dirt covering the floor. Most of the lumber in the stack had come from this tunnel. Turning to check the pile, he could see that some of the pieces had been worked into the stack from this side.

Puzzled, Raider moved into the tunnel, ducking occasionally to miss the overhead shoring. From the twists and turns, this shaft had closely followed a vein of silver. As in all of the abandoned workings, the track for the ore carts had been torn up for use elsewhere.

A hundred yards into the tunnel, he stopped, sniffing. Then he wet his forefinger and held it up, testing the air. There was a definite current, moving toward him. Another dozen paces, another corner turned, and the current of fresh air was strong enough to stir the flame and make the light flicker.

Suddenly the tunnel widened for the space of perhaps fifty feet. Raider stepped to the wall and held the light close; there was a mineral glitter in the rock, and a number of ore fragments littered the floor. Some of the cuts looked fresh. The fifty-foot section was perhaps five feet wider than the tunnel itself.

"Somebody's been working this section," Raider said, musing out loud. "Sonofabitch, another vein— and a goddamn rich one!"

The new vein was no more than twenty inches from the original wall of the shaft; might have come even closer to the surface. The veins could only have been inches apart. But that was the luck of mining. A man couldn't take apart a mountain rock by rock to steal its treasures, and this wouldn't be the first time that a fortune had been overlooked when it was almost begging to be taken.

Excited, Raider moved on another hundred yards, rounding another bend—and suddenly the shoring stopped. But the air current was much stronger, and now the temperature was rising. He pushed on, ducking to meet the lowering ceiling and working his way around boulders that had been too much trouble to remove. Soon there came a difference in the walls of the shaft, the roof of the tunnel rising again until it was almost high enough for Raider to stand erect. Every

now and then a fallen piece of ore said that the unknown parties who were highballing the Queen's silver
had come this way.

The shaft curved again, and this time Raider saw
daylight at the end. He fell back, turning down the
flame until the lantern flickered out, and stuck it behind a convenient boulder. Then he drew his Remington and moved on, cautiously, pausing every few paces
to listen. If the highballers were camped outside, they
wouldn't be pleased to see him suddenly appear.

He heard nothing. The last fifty feet of the tunnel
suddenly rose into a natural cavern, the roof a good
twenty feet over his head; then the cave narrowed
down to the mouth. The working shaft had broken into
the back of this natural cave, which had then been left
as a ventilator.

Raider crept to the entrance, where sunlight filtered
through a screen of covering brush. He peered out and
recognized the canyon where Zach had brought him up
to the town. At this point, he was a good half mile
below the lowest buildings of Coffin Canyon. The canyon itself was a good thirty feet below the cave, but
there was an easy path down. Raider smiled and removed his hat to wipe sweat from his brow.

"Zach, you goddamn old outlaw!" he said admir-
ingly. "You've been stealing the Queen's silver right
from under the Coffins' noses."

And then, down the canyon, he caught a moving
speck. Raider shaded his eyes, but the object was gone.
Not thinking twice, he holstered the gun and slipped
and slid down the trail to the canyon, pursuing the
thing he had seen on foot. He was moving faster;
within twenty minutes, he had caught up, ready to call
out—

"Hold it right there, mister!"

"Oh, hell!" Hands in the air, Raider turned around

to see Zach Gilchrist hunkered down behind a rock with his Henry. "Goddamn it, Zach, it's me!"

"O'Toole?" A look of disgust broke across the old man's features. "Goddamn it, you scared the bejesus out of me. What the Sam Hill you come up on me like that fer?"

"I might have a question or two of my own," said Raider. "Like, what were you doing in that abandoned shaft back there at the Queen?"

"Shit, that was you?" Zach lowered the rifle and came out from cover. "If'n I'd knowed that, I'da stayed fer you. I thought it might be them other fellers comin' back."

"What other fellers?"

The old man studied Raider for a minute, working a chaw of tobacco in his cheek. Then he spat and turned to start back up the canyon.

"C'mon, O'Toole," he said with a jerk of his head. "See fer yerself."

Raider watched him for a minute; then he shrugged and followed. It took almost twice as long to regain the distance. Zach plodded at a set pace, and then he pulled himself up hand over hand, using holds that Raider didn't even see, until he was back in the cave. During the past forty minutes, his only responses to Raider's questions had been uncommunicative grunts, but now he stood in the center of the cavern, hands on his hips.

"I heerd you back in the tunnel," he said. "Never figgered it might be you. Over here."

Raider followed Zach across the cave to what was almost a side chamber he had missed before. Zach picked up a lantern and lit it, holding it high to show a canvas-covered stack against the wall. The paulin cover was treated to be waterproof—tar-paulins, they were sometimes called.

"What is it?" asked Raider.

"Look fer yerself."

The canvas wasn't tied down. Raider caught an edge and threw it back to see stacked beneath it a dozen cases of dynamite.

"That stuff wasn't there five days ago, O'Toole," said Zach soberly.

CHAPTER EIGHTEEN

At dusk, the yard of the Coffin Queen was ablaze with light, although populated only by Raider's guards. He made a last check and then headed for the nearest saloon. The streets were filled with idled miners, and the bar was crowded, although conversation was muted, given only to one subject.

Raider slaked his thirst with beer, eying the crowd. Occasionally an argument or a fist fight flared, but it was quickly over. Despite the influx of customers, the saloon keepers remained unhappy with the condition of their cash boxes. Beer and the free lunch were the only items moving, nickels paid out grudgingly.

He left and crossed the street to the general store, which was just getting ready to close. Doc sat in a chair on the store's porch, foot propped against the hitching rail as he nursed an unlit stogie.

"Would you have a match, friend?" he asked, maintaining the masquerade that he didn't know Raider. The latter dug out a lucifer, scratched it on the nearest post, and cupped it while Doc sucked the cigar into life.

"Thank you," he said, exhaling with satisfaction.

"We gotta talk, Doc," said Raider.

"No time like the present." Doc waved a hand at a casual acquaintance who came out of the store. "Have you learned something?"

"I guess." He proceeded to relate his explorations. "Zach ain't the only one knows about that back door to the mine. That much dynamite could cause a hell of a mess with the workin' equipment, Doc. Collapse the

132

main shaft and destroy a lot of machinery. Probably trap the whole damn shift underground."

Doc rotated the stogie to get rid of a hot spot. "Zachariah Gilchrist has a way of reappearing in this matter, Raider."

"Zach's small potatoes, Doc. Besides, the Coffins don't even know that vein exists, so Zach doesn't look at it as stealin'. He told me today was the first time he's been back in the mine since he took me off the ledge, and when he found the dynamite, he skedaddled."

"Do you think this ties into the murder of John Williams?"

"Makes sense. The dynamite people obviously have men planted in the work crew. I figger Williams saw one of them where he shouldn't be or doin' something suspicious, and followed him."

"And was caught."

"Bushwhacked, more like it."

Doc sighed. "And there's still nothing to tell us who is behind all of this."

"Maybe not. But findin' the dynamite proves they're steppin' up activity. Except that maybe closin' the mine will serve the same purpose."

"Any suggestions?" asked Doc.

"Put a watch on the cave. Post somebody in the canyon to see who comes and follow them home."

"I don't like it." Doc shook his head. "Too iffy— you're assuming they'll be back right away, when they might not show for some time. After all, the dynamite could have been cached a week or more ago. Or even been there all along, but Zach just didn't stumble on it—you said it was in a side chamber. Besides, there's just the two of us to stand guard."

"Hell, we can have all the men we want!"

"But how many of them can you say aren't already mixed up in this affair, one way or another? No, I think we better keep this to ourselves a bit longer."

"You're not going to tell Junius?"

"Not if I can help it."

Disgusted, although he couldn't say why, Raider hacked to clear his throat and rolled a cigarette. When it was burning evenly, he said, "At least this proves you were wrong about them hidin' the silver inside the mine."

"It's still a possibility," Doc said mildly. "You haven't checked all of the abandoned shafts."

"I've done all the crawlin' around on all fours I intend," said Raider. "My throat is still caked with dust, and right now, I'm building a powerful thirst."

He hitched up his gun belt, eye on the saloon again. Doc got to his feet, chucking his cigar into the street.

"Stick to beer," he said. "I've a feeling things are going to happen pretty damn fast, so stay alert."

Raider snorted and took his leave, crossing the street again. Doc watched him until he disappeared into the Silver Bucket, and then he set out himself, heading for the big house. The moon was full, the sky a velvet blanket spangled with bright silver chips, but the evening insects were out, ready to attack any human whose stink wasn't powerful enough to kill them on the wing.

Despite the bugs, Helena was on the porch, waving a bamboo fan. Doc didn't see her until he was halfway up the steps, and then it was too late. She called him over to sit with her on the swing.

"It's so warm," she said. "I just couldn't stand being inside another minute. I do wish I could go for a ride to cool off."

"The mountain roads are dangerous after dark," said Doc.

"Yes, I know." Another sigh was followed by the sharp slap of her hand against the back of her neck. "Doctor, I'm worried about CeeCee."

"Anything in particular?" asked Doc.

"His lapses of memory. They seem to be coming

more frequently. This morning, he thought I was his first wife."

"He is an old man," said Doc.

"Senile, you mean. How much worse will it get?"

Doc shrugged. "It's hard to say. He seems to be in generally good health, although undoubtedly he suffers from hardening of the arteries. He may go on as he is for many years, and then again, he may suffer a stroke that will disable him, perhaps leave him bedridden. In that case, he'll need constant attention."

Helena did not try to suppress a shudder. And then she quickly added, "I'm sorry—you must think I'm a terribly callous person. But I'm no good around illness, Doctor. I've never had anything worse than winter sniffles, and I can't stand to see others become sick."

There was much Doc could have said, but he held his words. A moment later, he ventured, "There does seem to be something troubling him."

"Who? Oh, CeeCee." She laughed nervously. "What has he been saying?"

"That someone is trying to steal his silver."

Helena sat perfectly still for so long that Doc peered at her closely. Her jaw was set, and her knuckles were white where they gripped her fan. And then she uttered an almost imperceptible sigh.

"CeeCee still thinks he owns the mine. He insists it was stolen from him. To humor him, Doctor, I've written a lawyer who is checking to make sure that everything was done in a perfectly legal manner. Which I am quite certain it was," she added, just a shade too quickly.

"I thought it might have been because of the robberies of the silver shipments."

"I doubt he knows anything about them."

"I'm sure he doesn't," agreed Doc. "However, there is idle-talk making the round of the saloons . . ."

"What sort of talk?" she asked, interest picking up.

"Oh, really foolishness," said Doc, waving a hand.

"That CeeCee himself might be behind the robberies, trying to get back what he thinks is rightfully his."

There had been no such talk, of course; not until this minute, when he had been struck by the inspiration. But Helena uttered a forced laugh and began to wave her fan a bit too wildly.

"What a preposterous notion!"

"I agree," said Doc smoothly. "But it is understandable. After all, he was man enough to take a second wife."

"I know what you're thinking," Helena said, bitterness coming into her voice for the first time. "What they're all thinking," she added, waving her hand in the direction of the town. "That I married CeeCee for his money. Well, what if I did?"

Suddenly she turned to Doc and put her free hand on his arm. The swing had been moving slightly, but now Helena put her foot down and stopped the motion.

"I'm not a young woman, Doctor. I have two grown daughters of my own to watch out for. Yes, I married CeeCee for his money—I owed it to Moravia and Zelzah. People don't understand what it is to be a woman, with responsibilities but without resources except for those granted to her sex by God. And a fool's bargain it was!"

Doc felt acutely embarrassed by Helena's revelations, but he knew he had to listen and learn everything she had to tell him about the Coffin family.

"He has no money of his own?" he asked.

"Not a dime," said Helena harshly. "Euchred him out of everything, including his back teeth, did those precious sons of his! 'Sign over everything, Papa dear, and we'll take care of you for the rest of your life.' Jasper takes care of the bills at the office, pays the wages of the servants. When I married CeeCee, I was informed that I would be granted a reasonable allowance for clothing for myself and for the girls, but I have to submit every request for a new corset cover to him first! It's unbearable!"

The door opened and Zelzah came out, wearing a light wrapper and little else. Doc could see the upward curve of her breast against the light that came from the foyer. She peered suspiciously into the darkness that shrouded the swing until her eyes adjusted and she recognized Doc.

"Oh, Dr. Weatherbee! A telegram came for you a little while ago." She turned back a moment and came out with a fairly bulky envelope that Doc accepted, standing.

"Thank you, Zelzah."

"It's my pleasure," murmured the girl, posing provocatively despite her mother's indrawn snort of derision. "I've been meaning to ask you, Doctor—the other day I saw you talking to that John O'Toole. Do you know him well?"

"O'Toole?" Doc stirred, surprised. He had not been aware that any of the household had seen one of his brief meetings with Raider. He wondered if the servants in Junius' house had been talking out of turn.

"Why no," he said, thinking quickly. "I can't say I know the man at all. Which one is he?"

"You know, the tall one who is head of the guard force at the mine."

"That narrows it some," said Doc, forcing a smile. "But I don't think I know him. Would you like me to give him a message if we cross paths?"

"Oh, no," said Zelzah. She turned away to lean against the post with a sigh. "Oh, bother, I hate it when it's so hot! I wish I could go for a swim."

"Zelzah!" her mother snapped. "Young ladies of breeding do not swim!"

"Oh, pooh, Mama! You should try it sometime—it's ever so refreshing. But I forget, you are so old-fashioned about such things."

With that, she went back into the house, pouting. It

was clear that Raider had managed to make the acquaintance of the girls, but why hadn't he mentioned
the fact? Doc was pondering the significance of her
questions when a man turned into the yard of the house
and came up the steps. Doc stood, recognizing one of
the guards from the mine.

"Weatherbee?" He peered toward Doc. "Junius Coffin wants to see you right away. He wants John O'Toole,
too. You seen him?"

Doc scowled, aware of Helena's sudden stir of interest. He shook his head as she came to her feet.

"Try the saloons."

"Yeah," said the guard. He went on his way, and
Helena grabbed Doc's arm, her fingers digging like steel
claws into his flesh.

"Who are you?" she demanded harshly. "What are
you—a spy for Junius? Did he bring you here to spy
on me?"

CHAPTER NINETEEN

Doc broke free of Helena's grip, peeling her fingers off one by one. He cursed Junius for blowing his cover, but he realized that something serious must have happened.

"I'm not a spy," he lied. "Look, Helena, I have to go. I promise you, we'll talk—as soon as I can."

"You are a spy," she said coldly. "I should have known—it was so convenient, meeting you in Virginia City. How long has Junius had you tracking me? I suppose you've found out enough to satisfy his curiosity."

"We'll talk later," said Doc hastily. "When I return."

"Don't come back to this house! I may be forced to suffer the charity of my husband's sons, but I don't have to tolerate their informant under my roof! I'll send your bags to the hotel."

Doc surrendered with a shrug. "I'll take them now, and save you the trouble."

Helena moved toward the door, and for a moment he thought she intended to stop him from entering the house. Then she let out the air in her lungs with a long, heavy sigh and moved out of the way. He hurried up to his room, packed hastily, and came back down again to find Helena standing at the far end of the porch.

She heard him, but she did not turn around. Doc searched for something to say; then he shook his head and hurried down the steps. Instead of heading for the mine office, he turned toward the livery stable, where he deposited his bags in the wagon. After feeding Judith a sugar cube, he retraced his steps, answering Junius' summons.

The two men guarding the office door wouldn't let Doc pass until they sent in his name. The outer office was empty, although a dozen lamps burned, turning night into day. He rapped on the closed panel, and Jasper opened the door.

The three brothers were present, Jonathan looking harried, although reasonably sober. There was a fourth man, middle-aged, rawboned and dusty from traveling. He looked up from the glass of whisky he had been drinking to cut the dust in his throat.

"You wanted to see me?" Doc eyed the stranger carefully. He wore a well-cut suit of eastern style, but despite his dandyish appearance, his ruddy complexion said he was no stranger to the out-of-doors.

Junius stared at Doc, something very close to despair on his face. He was sprawled at his desk, his collar open and his hair disheveled. Before he could answer Doc's question, Raider arrived, pushing into the office without knocking. His eyes widened as he saw Doc, and then he took in the tension in the room.

"This is Philip Gibbons," said Junius tersely. "From Philadelphia. He just came in on the stage, with an offer for the Queen."

Gibbons returned the stares from Doc and Raider, clearly wondering what role they had to play in this game. Then he tossed off his whisky neatly, letting Junius do the speaking. Doc's eyes touched Jasper and Jonathan before returning to the oldest brother.

"A fair offer?"

"If you call eight cents on the dollar fair!" said Jasper bitterly.

"Gentlemen!" protested Gibbons. "I came in good faith, bringing what my principals consider an honorable offer for the Queen and its properties. We understand that you may feel that our offer undervalues the Queen, and we're open to negotiation. But please, let us not have rancor at the very beginning of our discussions."

He was soft-spoken, but there was the hint of steel in his voice. He walked across the room and helped himself to another glass of Junius' whisky; watching him, Raider knew that Gibbons was used to wearing a gun. Without it, he tilted to the right to compensate.

"Who are your principals?" asked Doc.

Raising an eyebrow, Gibbons looked at Junius, who answered: "Wincox and Company, an eastern syndicate."

"Do you know them?" asked Doc, thinking of his own cover story while in Virginia City.

"They're well known," said Jasper, "although until now they've mainly operated in Montana, and around Leadville."

"This is our first venture in the Sierras," confirmed Gibbons.

"Why the Queen?" asked Doc, taking the lead. The brothers seemed too stunned to speak.

"We've surveyed a number of likely prospects in the district. The Queen is the only really independent outfit around. And, gentlemen, the producers are facing a silver market that is rapidly becoming glutted."

"Then why do you want the Queen?" asked Raider.

"To hold for the future. And we're talking about ten or twenty years. For the present, we will cut back on production, dig just enough silver to satisfy the contracts already held. My principals are well connected in Washington, and I don't need to tell you that there's strong agitation to repeal Bland-Allison. We're betting it is repealed."

"If that happens," said Jasper dully, "silver will collapse. A lot of the producers will be forced to close down. Some of them for good."

"Including us," said Jonathan harshly. He scowled at the empty glass in his hand and then stood and remedied that condition, continuing: "We can't fight the bastards—everybody knows who'll have production sewed up. I say sell, and get out while there's still time."

"Not at eight cents on the dollar!" protested Jasper.

"Better eight cents than a penny on the dollar!" said Jonathan. Gibbons nodded.

"One vote for selling," he said, "and one against."

Junius shook his head. "You're at the hotel, Gibbons?"

"Yes, until I can find something better. You have a great deal of talking to do, gentlemen. I'll be waiting on your pleasure."

He touched his finger to the brim of his hat and left. As soon as the door closed, Jasper and Jonathan broke into an argument. Raider helped himself to the whisky, while Doc watched Junius, who listened to the squabble for perhaps a minute. Then he stood and suddenly bellowed:

"Shut up, you damn fools! Shut up and give me a chance to think!"

"We can't sell!" said Jasper. "They'll put us out of business, Junius. We won't have enough money to—"

"I said shut up!"

The second explosion was enough to cut off Jasper in mid-sentence, to Doc's regret. He was sure Jasper had been about to let something slip. Instead, he found Junius' wrath turned against himself.

"There's no more time for bullshit, Weatherbee," Junius said. "I want to know just where we stand, just how close you are to solving this mess."

"Closer than this morning," said Doc evenly. "Not close enough to name names."

"You have suspicions?"

"Yes, but that's all. I need a little more time."

"Time we no longer have," said Junius. He looked at his brother. "Jasper, what's the latest on the contracts?"

"Three more cancellations," he replied unhappily.

"Unless we can resume deliveries within the next couple of weeks, we'll lose most of what's left."

"It's a damn good thing the men walked out this morning," said Jonathan. "The San Francisco banks have shut off our credit—we can just about make one more payroll. I say sell, while we can still come out with whole skins."

"These Wincox people," said Raider. "You think they might be behind your troubles?"

"Who the hell knows?" said Junius. "The syndicate is legitimate, but Wincox is no more honest than he has to be. He was part of the Jay Gould–Jim Fiske syndicate that watered the stock of the Erie railroad. You know the story?"

"Yes," said Doc. "Commodore Vanderbilt thought he was buying control, but Fiske and Gould were printing fresh stock certificates so fast that some were still wet when they were transferred to Vanderbilt's brokers."

"They took the commodore for millions," said Junius. "So if shenanigans are involved, then Wincox could be mixed up in it. On the other hand, it's possible he just heard about our troubles and is taking advantage of the opportunity. It's for sure I believe Gibbons when he says the offer won't stay open."

"How much time did he give you?" asked Doc.

"Gibbons is leaving in forty-eight hours, with or without our answer."

"Can you stall him?"

Junius shrugged. "Not for long. What's the point?"

"I think we're close to breaking this thing," said Doc. "Forty-eight hours might even be enough, but try to stall for a few more days."

"Why the hell should we give you more time?" demanded Jonathan angrily. "You've had weeks, the pair of you, and you haven't managed to come up with one goddamn name or one solid bit of information."

"I agree," said Jasper suddenly, throwing his support to Jonathan. "If you have a lead, tell us. We have a right to know anything you've learned."

Doc glanced at Raider, who showed his disgust with the entire Coffin family when he shrugged.

"Let them sell out," he said. "I've only been shot at, shot up, and bounced halfway down a goddamn mountain. What the hell, they don't owe me any more than they do those poor bastards who died tryin' to deliver the silver, and the dumb sonsabitches who died in the mine."

"Seventy-two hours," said Doc. "You can give us that much time. Wincox will stall that long."

The brothers exchanged silent communication, and Raider shook his head and poured himself another three fingers of whisky. He tossed it down while Junius uttered another sigh, suddenly seeming as old as his father.

"All right, seventy-two hours. Starting now."

"Fair enough," said Doc.

He left the office, Raider at his heels. His partner said nothing until they were out of the yard, and then he let loose with a stream of obscenities that would have curled the hair of an innocent.

Doc listened patiently until Raider ran down and stopped for breath. They passed the big house, but the porch swing was empty. A lamp was lit in Helena's room, and the unmistakable figure of CeeCee appeared at his window, looking down into the darkness.

"Well?" demanded Raider. "I suppose you got some bright idea about pullin' a rabbit out of a hat, but I wish you'd let me in on it."

"You're going to keep an eye on Helena," said Doc.

Raider scratched behind his ear, surprised. "You think she's involved, Doc? She doesn't strike me as the cold-blooded sort. Remember, there've been a lot of good men killed."

"She has ice for a heart," said Doc soberly. He told Raider about the earlier confrontation with Helena.

"You think Mrs. Gaffney has room in the boarding-house?"

"Not right now, Doc. You want to bunk in with me?"

Neither partner thought too much of that idea, and Raider was relieved when Doc said, "No. I'll sleep in the wagon tonight. I've been neglecting Judith. I think maybe I'll hitch up and head out of town in the morning."

"And what do I do?"

"Helena goes for a ride every day after dinner—she calls it lunch. She says CeeCee gives her a headache if she doesn't get away from him. She varies her route, but tomorrow I think you should follow her. See if maybe she meets someone."

"Sounds to me like a long shot, Doc. What'll we do if this doesn't pan out?"

"Try something else," said Doc soberly. They had reached the livery. He turned in without saying good night, looking forward to the chance to spend some time with Judith. She might be only a mule, but right now she would make better company than any of the Coffins, or even Raider.

Doc had an instinct that rarely failed, Raider reflected as he headed for the boardinghouse, so most likely he was right in suspecting Madame Helena. Thinking of the woman brought the Riley girls into mind, and that made Raider randy. He considered paying a visit to one of the girls at the Silver Bucket but decided against it. That would lead to drinking, and tomorrow he wanted to be cold sober. He wanted to be ready for whatever happened.

Particularly if it happened right under him.

CHAPTER TWENTY

Raider was on the porch of the mine office when Helena von Dorf Coffin came out of the big house, a wicker basket on her arm. Most of the house was blocked by the mountain of tailings, but the front was visible. In his early days as boss, CeeCee had liked to watch the Queen from his front porch and his bedroom window.

Ambling, to give anyone watching the idea that he was bored with the patrol, he angled toward the street as she drove by in a light rig. He was in time to see her turn south on the Meadows road. Helena had a climb to the 9,000-foot level ahead of her, but the route was a favorite of Sunday picnickers. On a day like today, the likelihood was slim that she'd be sharing her ride with locals.

Raider's horse was tied at the office, a black that he still had not befriended completely. He spoke gently to the animal, stroking its neck before he mounted.

"Hold on, fella. We may have some work to do today, so let's not start out with the usual bullshit."

The horse answered with a short snort, flicking its ears, but it cooperated as Raider untied the reins and swung aboard. By the time they left the yard, the rig was just passing out of sight around a curve.

"Good," said Raider, soothing the horse's temperament by speaking softly. "She's committed, so we can hang back and let her get a lead."

It was a scorcher, and flies soon clouded around both Raider's head and that of the horse, attracted by their body stinks. The sky was cloudless, offering no relief. The climb up started as soon as they were out of the town, and within a mile, Raider used his bandana for the first time to mop up the sweat trickling down his neck.

It was an easy trail to follow, the rig raising a cloud of dust as he moved up until less than half a mile separated them. For a time, the climb grew steeper; then it leveled out again. The horse moved easily, even in the thin air. The surrounding peaks were still snow-capped.

Raider hoped Doc was right, although his own instincts said otherwise. But time was running out; less than sixty hours of Junius's begrudged allowance remained. Somehow they had to raise enough hell to get the other side goosed into action. For himself, Raider would have bet his bottom dollar and his saddle to boot that Wincox's sudden appearance was no coincidence.

The road leveled suddenly, heading across a flat shoulder of the mountain, straight as an arrow. The rig picked up a bit of speed, although Helena showed no sign of being in a hurry. But all she had to do was turn around, and she would see Raider

Raider cut away from the road and moved into a sparse wood that would shield him from Helena's sight if she turned around. Here, he began to pick his way higher on the flank of the mountain. Helena kept moving, passing several small meadows that were perfect picnic spots, if that was why she was here. He lost sight of her from time to time, paralleling the road, but picked her up again within a few minutes.

The trees grew thicker. The horse slowed its pace, picking a careful way; then it stopped. Cursing, Raider kicked his heels into the animal's flanks, but it tossed its head, snorting again, and refused to go any farther.

"Shit! You dumb sonofabitch! If there's anything dumber 'n a goddamn horse—"

Muttering, he swung down and pushed through the

underbrush—and found himself looking down a hundred-foot drop. The hollow below was treeless, but littered with broken rocks and boulders. The road was completely blocked off by lodgepole pine.

Raider moved back quickly, kicking a handful of pebbles over the edge. They rattled all the way to the rocks below. The horse had more sense than he.

"Sorry, boy," he said. Holding the reins, he picked his way down, several times nearly sliding on the carpet of pine needles. At last they broke out of the trees and spotted the road again.

But there was no sign of the rig. He remounted and started after her, cursing again. He knew what Doc would say if he lost Helena. He cut back almost to the road before he could see far enough ahead, but there was no sign of the dust cloud hanging.

"Shit!" he said again. "Where the hell is she?"

The horse made a noise, tossing its head, as though commenting on the stupidity of humans. Raider urged his mount forward, cautiously, still avoiding the road. Despite the heat of the sun, there was unmelted snow among the trees, and the air he breathed was crisp, cutting into his lungs.

Suddenly, the meadow opened. Raider almost blundered out of the cover of the trees before he spotted the carriage, pulled off the road beside a flat table rock. Beside it was a saddled horse, reins dragging on the ground. But there was no sign of the rider, or of Helena.

Raider quickly moved back into the woods and dismounted, tying the reins to a sapling. He drew his Remington, checking the action and the load. Then he holstered it again as he slipped through the trees, leather safety strap loose for a quick draw. Despite his hurry, he moved noiselessly, aware that the crack of a twig or the flight of a bird might reveal his presence.

He heard their voices before he saw them, although

he couldn't make out the words. Then he stopped, no more than a hundred feet away.

Helena sat in a natural seat on the back side of the table rock, the wicker basket at her feet. The basket was open, but whatever it had held had already been handed over to the man.

Raider studied him carefully, remembering the Riley girls' suspicions about these daily rides. The man hardly seemed the lover type. He had a mean face that sported a week's growth of beard, and he carried two pistols. His clothes were dirty, which meant that he probably wasn't too fastidious about his own care.

"The boys are ready to move," he said. "Gettin' anxious, in fact. They want to be paid off."

"They'll just have to wait," said Helena. "Tell them it won't be long now."

"I been tellin' 'em that," he said roughly. "They're tired of hearin' it. Some of 'em might get the idea of loadin' up and takin' off."

"They'll wait until I tell them to move," said Helena coldly. "I'm not going to have them jeopardize everything at this point. You get back to Brannigan's, and you keep them settled down."

"I'll tell them," he said glumly. "But I ain't promisin' they'll do it."

With that, he walked back to his horse, mounted, and angrily spurred it into a run that carried it in the opposite direction. But Helena did not move. Instead, she remained seated, staring across the meadow, lost in her own thoughts while Raider chafed in the woods.

Perhaps ten minutes passed, although to Raider it seemed more like an hour. Then Helena drew a silver flask from the basket and unscrewed the cap, tilting her head for a deep drink. She gasped, lowered the flask, and wiped her mouth with a handkerchief from her sleeve. Then she carefully replaced the cap, put the flask back in the basket, stood, brushing off her skirt, and carried the basket back to the rig.

She wasted no time in stowing the basket and climbing back into the rig. Raider gave her just enough time to turn the horse back toward Coffin Canyon before he mounted his own animal. For the first half mile he stayed in the big meadow, skirting the table rock, to avoid raising a dust trail. Then he moved back to the road and urged the horse into a run.

The gunman had a fifteen-minute head start, and was in a hurry himself. But within a mile the road turned down again, starting down the far side of the mountain. Raider came to an advantage point that let him see the road switching back and forth toward the valley far below. And perhaps three miles ahead, he spotted dust.

"That's him!" he said, patting the horse's neck. "Now let's see if you're as good as that liveryman claimed, horse!"

He spurred the horse, and the animal moved out easily. Now it was a matter of cutting the lead. But the gunman had a double advantage: he was going fast over a road he knew, and he knew just where he was heading. Raider could only follow, hoping the other didn't turn off somewhere ahead on a rocky surface.

The valley below seemed to be pure wilderness as Raider let the horse find its own best pace. He wished he had taken time to find out where the road would take him. He could see no ranches, no cabins, no sign of mining. At places, the road was scarcely a trail. The rigs from Coffin Canyon came up to the meadows, but there was nothing to show that any wagon had ever come down this side of the mountain.

Within an hour, however, it was clear that the road was swinging back toward the north and would eventually head toward civilization. He never caught sight of his quarry after the first time, but there was sign to mark his trail: a steaming horse biscuit here, fresh broken brush there. And there were no other roads leading off.

It was two in the afternoon when Raider left the meadow. Three hours later, he knew he was no more than half a mile behind the rider as the road rounded the curve of the mountain and came out into a valley. He reined up at a place where he could study the ranch that sat at the mouth of the valley, a substantial spread with half a dozen buildings, including a large barn. The ranch was still four or five miles away, but even from here, he could see horses in the corral.

"That's where he's headin', horse," said Raider. "Ain't no place else for him to go."

The horse snorted, tossing its head in apparent agreement, and Raider let it move forward at a walking pace. In no hurry to reach the ranch, he stopped at a creek to let the horse drink and graze on the grass while he rinsed out his canteen and answered the call of nature. His kidneys felt distinctly better when he remounted and urged the horse into the walking pace again.

Dusk covered the floor of the valley when Raider came to the edge of the ranch, although the sun was still bright on the flanks of the more easterly mountains. Two hours had passed since he had first spotted the ranch. Now he stopped and dismounted, tying the horse within the last copse of trees.

The buildings were painted with red ochre, and he could smell the horses. The house was two stories, the rooms he could see on the first floor lit. Several times men came out on various errands, one to throw a pan of dishwater into the yard, two others heading for the barn. Wishing for a cigarette, Raider hunkered down, waiting for the darkness to become more complete.

The sky slowly purpled and became spangled with stars. The moon was already on the down-slide, a thick crescent that did not relieve the darkness. The copse slowly woke to night sounds: the susurrus of insects, a horned owl leaving its nest. Raider heard frogs in the distance. There must be a pond on the far side of the barn.

He hadn't heard the sound that worried him most: the bark of a dog. It didn't seem likely the ranch didn't have any of the animals, but he hoped they were in the house. He straightened, easing the kinks from his muscles, and began to move toward the house, the Remington filling his hand.

The corral came first. Raider froze by the fence as someone came out of the house and stood on the porch. Red coals glowed where the man's face should have been. A horse blew by Raider's side, shifting nervously at the unfamiliar smell, and passed its fear on to its fellows. The horses, twenty or more of them, good riding stock all, began to mill around as Raider dropped into a crouch.

No one came to investigate. The man sucked his cigar into bright life and then threw it away and began to fuss with his trousers. He took a leak from the porch, not a hundred feet from Raider, who gritted his teeth until the other was finished. He heard the man sigh with relief; then he turned and went back into the house.

Releasing his breath, Raider straightened and circled the corral. Then he broke into a crouching run that carried him toward the barn. The room off the porch was the kitchen; he had counted at least four or five men in the moment the door stood open. There was a bunkhouse as well, and as he moved along the wall of the barn, the door opened again, and five men came out, heading for it. One carried a kerosene lamp. They were laughing at a joke begun in the house.

There had been at least ten men in the raid on the silver wagon. Raider knew he had taken care of a few of them, but there was no way of telling how many were left. They might have received reinforcements, for that matter.

None of the lights in the house had been turned off.

Five men in the bunkhouse, an untold number in the house. The odds were not in his favor.

But it was the barn that interested Raider the most, and now he made his way to the corner and peered around. The big sliding doors were shut, but a small door was cut into the wall only a hand's breadth away. Thankful for the darkness, he backed toward it, trying to watch both house and bunkhouse, and tried the latch.

It lifted easily, and the door came open on greased hinges. As Raider slipped through and closed the door, he was hit by old stinks: dried manure, moldering hay in the loft above. But there were no animal sounds, apart from the scurrying of rats. Brannigan, if this were his ranch, didn't keep a milch cow for his family. If he had a family.

As Raider's eyes became adjusted to the darkness, he was able to make out something large and bulky just within the big doors. He moved closer, putting out his hand until he touched the door of the Concord coach. His instincts were right; this was the bunch that had taken the silver.

But the coach sat high on its springs. The silver had been removed. Raider slipped his pistol into the holster, risking a match. He held the cupped flame and moved around the coach, looking for a likely hiding place. Chances were the silver was in the house—nearly two hundred thousand dollars' worth, if all five shipments were intact.

Metal clicked against metal as a steel hammer was drawn back in a brass action. Raider stiffened and started to reach for his gun. But the match was in that hand, and suddenly the flame burned his thumb.

"Shit!" he said aloud.

"Freeze, asshole!" said the man who had been waiting for him.

Raider started to shift his weight, ready to throw himself away from the gunman; then a match flared, and a lantern came to dull life. There were two of them.

"Shit!" he said again, cursing his luck.

CHAPTER TWENTY-ONE

In mid-morning, Doc hitched Judith to the Studebaker and headed out of town. He wanted to give the mule a chance to stretch her legs after so many days in the stable; and he also wanted to hook into the telegraph and send an urgent message to Wagner, detailing everything that had gone wrong. The agency would not be happy. They did not like to be frozen out of a case once an investigation was begun.

Confinement tells on mules almost as much as it does on humans. Judith had been pleased to have Doc's company last night and was downright unhappy when he left to have breakfast at Wong Fat's. When he returned and led her out of the stall, she backed eagerly into the traces.

"I'm sorry, old girl," Doc said softly, feeding Judith a sugar cube and scratching her ears. "Feels like you've been in prison, doesn't it? The sooner we all show our heels to this two-bit burg, the happier we'll be."

Judith made a noise that might have been agreement as Doc mounted to the seat and took up the reins. There were a good many idlers on the street as he drove out of town. The miners were counting their dollars and hoarding their pennies.

A few had ridden out, giving up on the Queen and its management. For the most part, the quitters were loners, men with horses and bedrolls who would head for more promising territory at a curse from a foreman. Just outside of town, however, Doc passed one wagon loaded with household goods and what seemed like a dozen kids. He thought he recognized the miner who

155

was driving. The woman beside him never looked up as the brightly painted Studebaker rolled by, although the kids waved and shouted hello.

As the Studebaker rattled along, Doc settled himself to enjoy the day, letting his mind go blank. He had given up during the night on trying to pump fresh ideas out of stale information.

Within half an hour, the stage to Carson City passed Doc. He wondered idly if it were the coach involved in moving the silver from Graveyard Gap, but he dismissed the notion. The local stage line would send it north or east between the twice-weekly runs up to Coffin Canyon. There were no stages to Virginia City, which had the railroad.

An hour out of town, Doc began to eye the lone telegraph line. Half an hour later, he came to a place where the line suddenly cut straight down the side of the mountain, passing through a wooded knoll below. The route avoided a long S-shaped switchback that added a mile or more to the road.

A quarter-mile farther, Doc found a place to pull off that also gave easy access to the knoll. The taut wire was only a hundred yards away and ten feet overhead when it crossed the edge of the knoll. He tied the reins loosely, allowing Judith to graze on the fresh green grass, and climbed into the wagon to dig into the secret compartment in the bed.

First Doc brought out the jug of blue vitriol, handling the battery acid gingerly. He had splattered himself a score or more times over the last four years and ruined more than one good pair of trousers while setting up his telegraph key. Now he wore stout gloves while handling the vitriol.

The battery jars and the key followed, and the code book. When Doc had carried all to a spot just beneath the wire but concealed from the road above by an overhang, he went back and checked the condition of his Premo Senior camera and the portable equipment for developing the wet plates. As yet, there had been no need to take photographs, although they were essential to the final report.

None of the plates had broken or cracked. Satisfied, Doc went back and prepared his sending equipment, pouring the vitriol into the battery jars. He then tossed a wire over the telegraph line, securing it to make a taut connection, and hooked the key into the circuit. Then he opened the code book for a last-minute addition to the report he had composed and coded the night before.

The message went off quickly, reporting the decision of the Coffins to limit Doc's time and options drastically—not that he could honestly report anything concrete beyond the discovery of the dynamite. Done, he settled himself in a shady spot, knowing it would take time for the message to reach Chicago. He might be in for several hours of waiting before the key began to sing.

He removed his coat and folded it to make a pillow, tipped his hat over his eyes, and settled himself for a nap. There was nothing he could do in Coffin Canyon until Raider came back from tailing Helena—

Doc sat up, cursing. He had just remembered the telegram Zelzah had given him last night.

He jumped to his feet and headed for the wagon on a dead run. In the hurry of packing to leave CeeCee's house, he had stuffed the telegram in his carpetbag. Now he dug it out and ripped open the yellow envelope.

The message was from Denver: two pages, in code. He had left the code book back with the key. He retraced his steps and then had to come back to the wagon again for writing paper and a pencil. This time he settled himself on the seat to decode the message while Judith looked around, puzzlement on her face. It wasn't like Doc to be running back and forth like a child without purpose.

Five minutes later, the bulk of the message decoded, Doc stared dumbfounded at the pages in his hand. Now he had the long-awaited report on Helena Riley von Dorf Coffin. Helena Riley, legally. It seemed the lady had neglected to divorce her first husband, the father of her daughters, before tying the knot with the second —or with the third, the fourth, or any of the others.

Doc finished decoding the message, which said there had been a dozen husbands so far. Known husbands; it was quite likely there had been a few others not reported to one or another of the dozen law enforcement agencies who had compiled the information requested by the agency.

A dozen husbands in the seventeen years since she had walked out on Walter Riley without so much as a good-bye or a thank you, dear, for the contents of the cash box Helena had removed from the Riley Dry Goods Emporium in Philadelphia. She had headed north during the lucrative war years, had been recorded in New York, Boston, and several other New England cities. In between husbands, Helena practiced the oldest profession.

Madame Helena was a madam.

She had quickly been run out of Boston by the outraged blue bloods, and she had then made her way to Denver. The vast number of aliases was the reason it had taken so long to compile the information in the report. In Denver, she had kept the second most famous house after Mattie Silk's until Mattie had decided Helena was trying to make herself number one. Denver was a wide-open town, corrupt to the very meanest of public servants, but the police chief and the board of aldermen were on Mattie's payroll.

So Helena had moved on, to Coffin Canyon. With another change of name. Von Dorf was a penniless German count, a remittance man paid an allowance to stay on this side of the Atlantic. She had left the count after less than a week, sticking him with several thousand dollars' worth of bills.

What had brought her to Coffin Canyon was a matter for speculation. The report suggested that the heat had been too great in the cities, and so Helena had come looking for a quieter place to do business. It was assumed she had intended to buy one of the saloons and set herself up in business again, but something happened to change her plans: she had met CeeCee.

After rereading his notes for the third time, Doc folded them together with the original message and slipped them back into the envelope. The report mentioned the daughters only twice, saying that so far as known, they did not join in with any of Helena's business ventures. But they had to know what she was doing.

Doc cursed himself again for not having read this report the night before. This information had to be given to Junius right away. He jumped down from the wagon and began to gather his equipment, carefully pouring the vitriol from the jars back into the jug and stowing everything away. The return message would be rerouted to Coffin Canyon when he didn't answer with his private key.

Ten minutes later, he was on the road headed back to Coffin Canyon. The five miles they had come down in ninety minutes took two hours to retrace, and as he came into town, he spotted the familiar figure of Raider riding out in the other direction.

Doc thought of riding after him; then he decided it could wait. It was better to let him trail Helena to see just what she was about. There was still nothing to tie her in directly to the Queen's problems, although her outrage when she learned that CeeCee no longer controlled his mine must have been a sight to see.

He went straight to the mine office and insisted on being closeted alone with the eldest brother. He let Junius read the decoded report for himself, watching the blood suffuse his face as Junius built himself toward an apoplectic fit.

"By God, I'll have her arrested! Run out of town! I'll have her hung!"

"Not so fast," said Doc. "All you can prove is that she tried to swindle your father."

"Thank God the marriage is invalid!"

"Yes, but keep that news to yourself. I'm still not convinced that one of your brothers isn't involved in this in some way. And there's no evidence to tie Helena directly into the robberies."

"But you do believe she's behind them?"

"Involved in some way," said Doc. "I'm going to try and get back into her good graces."

"Gibbons was here an hour ago," said Junius. "Says he reported to his principals, and they demand an answer. He won't wait beyond forty-eight hours."

"He's pressuring you, which means that they're eager to make a deal. Tell him you've thought it over, and the answer is no. I'll wager he ups the offer."

"What do I tell Jasper and Jonathan?"

"As little as possible. Nothing of this report. If either one is working with her, he'll know the game is blown."

Junius shook his head. "I can't believe either of my brothers would try to destroy the Queen. After all, they share equally in the profits."

"But you run the mine," pointed out Doc. "And if Gibbons is right that Bland-Allison is about to be repealed, there'll be a lot of new ghost towns in the Sierras. A third of nothing is still nothing."

Junius sighed. "All right, Weatherbee. Do what you have to. But do it quickly."

Doc left the office and settled himself in a place where he could watch for the return of Madame Helena. His stomach reminded him that he had skipped lunch, but he did not want to risk taking the time to go downtown to Wong Fat's. His belly was touching his backbone when she at last appeared, over two hours later.

Doc followed her into the yard and remained unseen until she stepped down from the rig, taking the hand of her servant. She drew herself up to her full height when he stepped forward.

"I have nothing to say to you!" she said.

"But I have plenty to tell you," countered Doc. He glanced at the servant. "Alone. Please, I ask just a few minutes of your time."

He thought she was going to refuse, but Helena sniffed, tossed her head, and said haughtily, "Very well. You may have five minutes."

She carried the wicker picnic basket into the house and did not release it even when Doc followed her into the front parlor. He stepped to the sliding doors and checked the room to be sure that they could not be overheard, and then he started to take a seat. But Helena remained on her feet, and Doc caught himself and did the same.

"Your time is running out," she said coldly. "Say what you came to say."

"You were right," said Doc, choosing his words with care. "I am here under false pretenses—but not as a spy. I'm a Pinkerton agent."

CHAPTER TWENTY-TWO

Raider blinked as his eyes adjusted to the sudden flare of the lantern and let the Remington fall from his fingers. He studied the pair who had managed to get the drop on him.

The one with the lantern was only a boy, pimply-faced, with an idiotic, drooling grin. The other one was trouble: a hardcase in his thirties, sullen-faced and mean. The Colt .45 in his hand held steady on Raider's heart.

"Go tell Brannigan we got company."

The boy started to leave with the lantern, and the man cursed and called him back. "Leave the light, you damn fool! Hang it there on the post."

"Ah'm sorry, Jack," said the boy, backing away, the grin gone. "Ah'll git Brannigan right away, Ah will."

This wasn't the pair Raider had seen enter the barn; they had been inside only a few minutes before leaving again. Nor had these two been part of the bunkhouse group. Which meant they had been inside all along, waiting for him. A setup.

"Turn around," said Jack easily. "Git over there by the wall—that's close enough. Now lean forward and put your hands up as high as you can reach."

The position was awkward; off-balance, Raider could do nothing while Jack maintained a safe distance. Inside another minute, however, he heard voices and looked around as half a dozen men came through the little door, the boy bringing up the rear.

One was the man Raider had followed: a barrel-chested tough about forty. He still wore his guns. The man beside him was in his late fifties, but the younger man seemed to be in charge. Neither seemed pleased with company, expected or otherwise.

"I'm John O'Toole—"

"Shut up!" said the older man. "You speak when somebody tells you to open your mouth, mister." He looked at the other. "This the gun follered you down the mountain, Billy?"

"He's the one, Brannigan."

"There's been a misunderstanding—"

Before Raider could finish the sentence, Jack stepped forward and cracked him across the skull with the barrel of his gun. Raider swallowed a cry of pain and saw stars as the strength went out of his knees. He sagged and just kept himself from falling. Before he could pull himself up again, Jack holstered his pistol and came forward to run his hands over Raider's body and legs.

"Search him good," said Billy.

Raider shook his head to clear his clouded vision while Jack found the derringer tucked into the top of his boot and removed it, along with the sheathed knife from the other boot. He then checked Raider's pockets.

"What did you find?" asked Billy.

"Double eagle an' twelve dollars in other coin," said Jack. "Railroad watch an' makin's. That's all."

"Colby, git a rope and tie his hands behind his back. Give Brannigan the watch and the money, Jack. You can keep the makin's."

Jack didn't seem overjoyed with his bounty as he stuffed the tobacco pouch into his pocket and obeyed Billy's orders. Another man brought a worn length of lariat and tied Raider's wrists. The rope dug into the thin layer of flesh over his bones, burning. Raider automatically flexed his shoulders, testing the knot; Colby knew what he was doing. Only a knife would remove the bonds.

Then the man spun Raider around until he faced the

others and gave him a shove that sent him stumbling two paces forward. He almost tripped but caught himself in time to save a bit of his dignity. Billy, Brannigan, and the others eyed him, studying his face.

"Any of you boys know him?" asked Billy.

"I don't rightly know," said Colby, shaking his head. "Somethin' about him seems familiar, Billy, but I cain't rightly say what it is. The way he carries hisself, mebbe. I seen him someplace."

"I tried to tell you, I'm John O'Toole," said Raider. "If you'll give me a chance to explain—"

"All right," said Billy. "Talk."

"I'm looking for my extra horse," said Raider. "A roan gelding—I thought I saw him in the corral. I was just checkin' him out—"

"That's a lie!" said Jack. "That roan belongs to Pete Saugus—I been ridin' with Pete two year, Billy! He's had the roan all that time."

"Shut up!" said Billy, disgusted. "I know he's lyin'— I just want to hear his story. Mister, you been on my tail —I caught you clear against the sky three different times. You was right behind me when I rode in damn near three hour ago. If'n you had somethin' to say, or look at, you would've rode in then."

Raider shrugged. "You can't blame a man for bein' cautious."

Before Billy could say anything else, there was a commotion outside; a moment later, another man came in. He was carrying Raider's saddlebags.

"Had a bitch of a time findin' his horse, Billy," said the newcomer. "Darker 'n the inside of a whore's cunt out there."

"All right," said Billy. "Take him in the house, and call the other boys in, too. Mebbe one of them has seen this jasper before."

Raider was ready for the shove between the shoulder blades that sent him staggering forward. Two of the men went out first, drawing their pistols despite the fact that his hands were tied. Billy and the others followed. Raider saw his horse tied to the corral. The man who brought it hadn't unsaddled the animal.

For a few seconds, his mind spun with schemes to make a break for it. But it was all foolishness. He could do nothing, tied and surrounded by this many guns.

The boy was sent to the bunkhouse to summon the other members of the gang while Raider stumbled up two steps onto the porch and then into the kitchen. A large wood range against the far wall radiated heat, while two women, one Brannigan's age and the other a teenager, were almost finished washing up the supper dishes. The long, narrow kitchen held two tables shoved together end to end and an assortment of battered and broken furniture, including three love seats and a dozen chairs.

Somebody shoved a kitchen chair against Raider's legs and he sat down suddenly while Billy took the saddlebags, unstrapped them, and dumped the contents onto the table. He pawed through Raider's belongings and then unrolled the clean shirt and jeans to find the wallet.

Billy cast a glance at Raider when he made the discovery, but Raider kept his face perfectly blank. His stomach was churning, however, as Billy emptied the wallet.

"Three hundred dollars," he said, folding the paper money and stuffing it in his own pocket. None of the others said a word while he turned the wallet inside out, felt along the seams, and found one thicker than the others. Drawing a pocket knife, he cut open the seam and drew out the card that was concealed within.

"Well, now!" he said, reading the card. "Take a look at this, Brannigan."

"What is it, Billy?" asked the older man, coming over. He took the card and turned it over, but it was obvious he could not read. "What does it say?"

Before answering, Billy glanced at the women. "Git

them out of here," he said. "They ain't got no business hearin' what we're gonna say."

"All right, you heard Billy," said Brannigan, suddenly blustering. "Git, both of you!"

The older woman turned without a word and left the kitchen, browbeaten by her years with Brannigan, and by life itself. The girl, however, showed more spunk; she glared at Billy for almost five seconds before throwing down her dish towel.

And then, as she turned away, her gaze crossed Raider's and locked with his for an instant. He saw fire in the girl's expression and knew by the set of her jaw and by the stiff way she carried herself that she hated Brannigan and Billy alike.

Who was she? The girl seemed too young to be Brannigan's daughter, although the relationship wasn't impossible. The woman might be younger than she looked. But before Raider could speculate further, the door closed, and the men returned their attention to Brannigan as the five from the bunkhouse arrived.

That made fourteen, with Brannigan and the boy. Raider counted them again. A small army, although he thought he recognized only two or three from the gang that had ambushed the silver shipment. Some of the others might have been there as well, but with the phony Indian war paint they had worn, he couldn't be sure. He decided that Brannigan and the boy had not been along on the raid.

He did not like the way the newcomers were eying him. One came forward, squinting through myopic eyes, and actually picked up Raider's chin and forced him to look up.

"I know you," he said, his breath a foul stench that almost made Raider gag. "Yep, I never fergit a face. I know you, all right."

"From where?" asked Billy.

The man moved back a pace or two, scratching at a

louse under his armpit. "From the Coffin Queen—that there's John O'Toole, head of the guard detail."

Raider studied the man again but couldn't remember him. Perhaps he had been in town just during the last week or so, but he could very well have been working in the Queen, among the several hundred men who labored in the crushers or the smelters.

"Well, that's right interestin'," said Billy. "Only his name ain't John O'Toole, and the Queen ain't the only outfit payin' his wages. He's a Pinkerton."

The men stared at Raider for a moment, and then Colby stepped forward with a curse and swung his clubbed fist at Raider's head. The blow caught him alongside the jaw, loosening several teeth, and he tasted blood.

"You bastard!" cried Colby. "I oughta shoot you where you are, you no good cocksuckin' bastard!"

"Back off, Colby!"

Billy's order came an instant too late to save Raider from another smash in the face. This time Colby's knuckles caught the bridge of Raider's nose. For an instant, everything went numb; and then he felt blood trickling from one nostril. His head fell until his chin hit his chest, and more pain stabbed through his jaw.

"Let me shoot the bastard, Billy!" pleaded Colby. "You know the Pinks kilt my brother an' left my old man crippled fer life. I swore then I'd kill ever' Pink I could. Please, let me have him."

"Yer a damn fool!" said Brannigan. "Kill a Pinkerton and you'll be marked fer life—they'll hunt you down like a dog."

"Simmer down," said Billy. He looked thoughtful. "We ain't gonna kill him—at least, not yet. What I want to know is, how many more of them are there? Pinks never work alone."

He advanced on Raider. "How about it, Pink? How many more of you are there?"

"Enough," said Raider, pretending an assurance he

did not at the moment feel. "Brannigan's right—Allan Pinkerton and his boys will cross the world to find the man who kills an agent."

Billy scratched his head. The others stirred nervously. They didn't like the presence of a Pinkerton—not even one who was hog-tied and unable to do anything.

"A smart man would let me go," said Raider.

Billy laughed, and Raider shivered. There was no fear in that laughter. Billy was enjoying himself. He knew he was in control of this situation, and right now he was weighing Raider's value alive against the trouble he'd be worth dead. The scales were tipping the wrong way.

"I'm gonna let you live fer a while, Pink. A few more days, it won't matter one way or the other. Mulligan!"

"Yeah, Billy?" He was the scruffy one who had identified Raider.

"Yer goin' back to Coffin Canyon tonight."

"Shit, Billy!" he protested. "There ain't enough moon fer coyotes to fuck. I'll break my fool neck."

"Can't be helped. You gotta tell the boss what's happened. She don't know the Pinks are in on it. Tell her I gotta know whether we go ahead or back off."

Stilling further protest, Mulligan left. There was no longer any doubt in Raider's mind as to the involvement of Helena Coffin. He hoped Doc would be on the alert.

"What'll we do with him?" asked Brannigan, indicating Raider.

"Take him upstairs and tie him to a bed."

"You mind if I take a leak first?" asked Raider, coming to his feet. Billy laughed again, a hard sound, and pointed to Colby.

"Take him outside, Colby, but tie a noose around his neck first."

"What fer?" asked Colby, puzzled.

"So when you untie his hands he won't make a break for it, asshole!" said Jack, throwing Colby a lariat. "Or do you want to take it out and hold it for him?"

Colby scowled, but he made no reply as he obeyed the order. He pulled the noose tighter than necessary. Raider rasped for breath, but as they went outside, Colby gave him almost ten feet of lead and held his gun on Raider's back, the hammer cocked. He stood on the top step, flexing his fingers to work out the tension before he could undo his buttons. And when he finished, the noose was left in place while Colby and another took him upstairs to a bedroom and proceeded to tie him spread-eagled to the bed.

Coiling the lariat he had used to make the noose, Colby stood in the door for a moment, eyes narrowed with hatred.

"You ain't gittin' outa here alive, Pink!" he said. "Remember that, and fergit what Billy or anybody else says. Yer a dead man right now."

With that, he was gone, taking the light.

CHAPTER TWENTY-THREE

Helena studied Doc with hooded eyes. Her face was a careful blank, but the thumb of her right hand slid back and forth over a pinch of the fabric of her skirt, working in a little circle, betraying her shock.

"I see," she said after a moment. "I assume this means the boys hired you to find out what you could about me."

"You're wrong," said Doc easily. "The agency was brought in because of the silver thefts. I was in Virginia City to try and get a line on the robbers—it was coincidence that you happened to be there at the same time. I will say I was startled to learn your name."

"Are you really a doctor?"

"I have no formal degree, but I passed the Texas licensing examination. I'm sure I know as much about medicine as most of the charlatans who put parchment on their walls."

"You must admit, it seems strange that you appeared here, too."

"Remember," said Doc, "you were the one insisted I stay here, in this house."

Helena released her skirt and placed her hand on her breast. She took a deep breath and held it. When the air came out, the lines of her face had softened. Doc tried to read her new expression, but except for a sudden fire in her eyes, there was nothing to reveal the woman's inner feelings.

"It seems I've misjudged you," she said. "Please, accept my apology, Doctor."

"An honest mistake," said Doc, smiling. "Apology

accepted. You do understand that I could not tell you this before, Helena."

"But now you are free?"

"Not completely, but I'm trusting your discretion. I think we are close to discovering the identity of the man or men behind the robberies, but of course I'm not at liberty to say any more. At least, not just yet."

"Why have you told me this much?"

"Because I want to move back into this house. Here, I can keep an eye on . . . certain individuals."

"My husband?"

Doc parried the suggestion. "Do you suspect him of complicity in the robberies?"

"It's possible. CeeCee is a jealous man, Doctor. I know, at times he seems mad. At other times, however, he is quite the sanest man I've ever known."

"You're suggesting that he signed over his interest in the Queen in one of his bad periods?"

Rather than answer, Helena turned and walked to the window. She pulled aside the lace curtains to look out. From any of the rooms on the front or on this side of the house, the mountain of tailings outside the crusher building dominated the view. The man-made hill had grown in twenty years almost to dwarf the natural hill that rose above the mine. It was a depressing sight: half broken rock, half grayish sludge that was a mixture of mud and the clay that was always found with silver-bearing ore.

"I can understand why my husband's first wife hated this house," said Helena. "I hate the mine—hate this town. Why are you telling me this?"

Her voice was gentle, but as Helena let the curtain fall and turned back to Doc, he saw the hard glitter in her eyes. Knowing the extent of her criminal career, he didn't underestimate the woman; for a moment, Doc wondered if she had seen through his carefully spun fabric of half-truths.

The only things that didn't jibe with the report on

Helena's past and her present involvement with the attempt to wrest the Queen away from CeeCee's sons were the number of men killed in the ambush of the silver shipments, and the mine "accidents."

But Doc had met deadly women before. In his four years with Pinkerton's, he had come to realize that soft curves and a helpless manner could be put on as easily as a change of dress or a smile. Helena was smiling now, but underneath she remained one of the hardest women he had ever known. And she was striking into new territory. Perhaps her original intent had been to take CeeCee for every possible dollar and move on, leaving him just another man on a long list of bilked suckers. But now, frustrated in her first plans, she was striking for control of a major silver mine. Doc was sure that she was in someway involved with the Wincox syndicate; and as that thought popped in his mind, he decided to request a report on the leading officers of the syndicate, to see if there was a connection.

Still, things were rushing to a climax; it was unlikely such an investigation could be completed in time to help now. But curiosity compelled him to want to know the answer.

"I'm taking you into my confidence for two reasons," he said slowly. "First, it is important that I be free to come and go in this house. For that, I'll most likely be calling on you for help."

Helena smiled, but the hard glitter remained, turning her eyes into chunks of ice. She approached him and placed a hand on his wrist as her lips made a natural pout, ready to be kissed.

"You are an unusual man," she said throatily. "I've never known a detective before. I knew from the moment I saw you in Virginia City that there were . . . depths to your character that I wanted to plumb. And now that I know the truth, I find your presence . . . even more stirring . . ."

The lies came more and more easily to Doc's lips.

"I . . . think you're something special, too, Helena. I don't want you to think ill of me. I've never met a woman like you."

Wondering where CeeCee might be at this minute, Doc did what was expected: he kissed Helena. She clung to him longer than necessary, her fingers digging into his arms while the blood heated in his veins. His ears grew hot with embarrassment as he realized that another part of his body was ready for immediate action.

Helena broke away. "No . . . not now." She patted her lips with a scented handkerchief from her cuff. "We can't, now."

"You're right," said Doc, aware that his voice rasped. "We must be sensible, Helena. I'm sorry."

She let the apology stand, although she had initiated the action. Suddenly she took a chair, hands folded primly in her lap.

"How may I help?"

"Are you sure you want to involve yourself? There are desperate men mixed up in what's been happening, Helena. It could be dangerous."

"If my husband is behind these robberies, I want to help. Now, what can I do?"

Doc surrendered with feigned reluctance. "CeeCee goes out frequently for walks—I've seen him take the path that goes up the hill. Do you know where he goes?"

"Not precisely. CeeCee has a great deal of nervous energy, Doctor. There are paths and trails that go for miles through these hills. I offered to accompany him when we first married, but he prefers to walk alone. He said I was too slow for him."

"I'm going to post a man up in the hills to follow him. I want to know when he leaves."

"Do you think he meets . . . his accomplices?"

"It's possible," said Doc. Leaving his words hanging, he drew his watch. "I have to meet Junius and make arrangements to post the man on the hill. I hope matters are close to being settled, but I intend to light a couple of fires under chairs to push these people into action."

"Please," said Helena, standing again. "Don't do anything rash."

Doc smiled. "I have a healthy respect for my hide. I've managed to keep it whole and in good health this far, and I won't slack off now."

He turned and opened the sliding doors, quickly, as though half expecting to find an eavesdropper. The hall was empty, but he could hear CeeCee pacing upstairs. He left the house, aware that Helena was watching him from the parlor window. He resisted the impulse to wave at her as he headed for the mine office.

Helena watched Doc disappear and then let the lace curtain fall. Her eyes burned now as she turned to the wicker basket she had carried on her ride and dug into it. She came out with a small pistol. She held the gun easily, familiarly, her mouth set into a hard line.

Ten hours later, close to midnight, Doc settled himself for the night, his mind churning with worry. Where the hell was Raider? His partner should have been back hours ago, unless he had run into trouble. Doc had a sinking feeling that that was just what had happened.

But there was nothing he could do; Raider could be anywhere within fifty miles. Doc turned over and pounded his pillow into shape for the tenth time in five minutes; then he sat up. The air was too hot for sleeping even if he had been exhausted. A fly buzzed incessantly overhead while other insects came through the open window, attracted by the scent of human sweat.

In darkness, Doc drew on trousers and boots, hooked his suspenders over his shoulders, and fumbled for his cigars. Moving easily to avoid waking the house, he made his way down the stairs and out onto the porch.

The air was a trifle cooler although it was dead still. He found a wicker chair at the far end of the porch and sat, cheroot in his fingers, breathing deep of the night scents, listening to the night sounds. At last he wet the cigar and drew a match—

A footstep crunched.

Doc froze, hand ready to strike the match against a post. He saw a shadowy figure come into the yard. The man stopped by a live oak that had been here before the house was built but now was dying from the noxious smoke that came from the smelter. He whistled, softly. And then he repeated the whistle twice, five seconds between soft trills. It might have been the lonesome call of a night bird.

For several minutes, nothing happened. Doc tried to make himself small in his chair, wishing he had worn a dark shirt. And then he heard the creak of a riser within the house as someone came down the stairs.

"Who's there?" It was Helena, coming out onto the porch in her wrapper. The figure slipped out of the tree's shadow and came to the steps.

"Webster Mulligan, ma'am. Bartlett sent me."

"You fool! I told him never to come here!"

"It's real important, ma'am. We caught us a Pinkerton snoopin' around the ranch. Billy says he's gotta know whether to go ahead or back off."

Both Helena and Mulligan spoke softly. Doc strained to hear their words, missing half of what Mulligan said in his toothless mumble. But he didn't miss Helena's next sharp utterance:

"A Pinkerton? At Brannigan's?"

"Yes'm. He follered Billy down the back side of the mountain. Billy figgers he was on his trail all the way from the meaders an' his meetin' with you."

Helena cursed angrily. "What is his name?"

"I fergit his real name," said Mulligan, "but he's been callin' hisself John O'Toole—he's the one made head of the guard detail at the mine."

"I should have known there'd be more than one of them," said Helena bitterly.

"Billy wants to know what to do," said Mulligan again.

Helena pressed her fist against her teeth, thinking. Doc tried hard not to breathe; the cheroot had broken under the tension of his hands. He wished he had brought the Diamondback and gave silent thanks that the chair's wings concealed him from Helena's direct line of vision. He slowly lowered his hands to his lap and pressed the match into a fold of his trousers. He still held the broken cigar.

"Tell Bartlett to move everything up twenty-four hours," she finally said. "He's to start tomorrow evening."

"Yes'm," said Mulligan. "What about the Pinkerton?"

She shrugged. "Tell him to do whatever is necessary." And with that, she turned and went back into the house, clutching the wrapper, while Mulligan slipped away as quietly as he had come.

Doc tossed the cheroot over the porch rail and came to his feet, wiping his palms against his trousers. Raider had let himself be caught! Once again, Doc would have to pull his dumb partner out of the fire.

But at least he knew where he was. Brannigan's ranch; that was one of the ranches the farmer down on the flats had mentioned. In Blue Horse Canyon.

The question now was whether to call out a posse or to go after Raider by himself. Helena had ordered Bartlett to go into action the next evening. Doc was sure that action had something to do with the cache of dynamite. It was time to tell Junius everything, despite the late hour. Once the Coffins were on the alert, Doc could go after Raider.

He waited several more minutes, however, wanting to give Helena time to get back to her room. He sat and tugged off his boots; and when he thought ten minutes had passed, he went back into the house and picked his way up the stairs, staying to the side of the risers.

No light appeared under Helena's door, although if she were asleep, she was an even colder character than Doc had first believed. He picked his way down the hall to his room and slipped inside, carrying his boots; then he eased the door shut, holding the knob from turning until the striker hit the notch in the striker plate with a soft click. He started to cross the room—

A match flared, touching a lamp. He blinked and turned to see Helena. She stood by the dresser, a .32 in one hand and trained on Doc while she lowered the chimney on the lamp with her other hand.

"I knew you were on the porch," she said. "I smelled your cigar."

CHAPTER TWENTY-FOUR

Raider opened his eyes to pitch darkness, agonizing pain, and a sour taste in his mouth. For a minute, half-awake, he thought he was back in Zach's shack; and then he tried to move and shooting pains stabbed through his legs and his arms and across his back.

He stiffened, testing the bonds that held him to the bed. The bullet wound in his shoulder flared again, although it had been almost healed. There was no slack in the ropes, and to top off the other annoyances, his feet burned in his boots as though someone had set his socks on fire.

A hand touched his arm.

Raider stopped breathing for an instant, blinking against the darkness. The touch was light, gentle. He tried to lick his lips, tried to spit away the crud stuck to his swollen tongue.

"Who is it?" His voice rasped. "Who's there?"

A vaguely grayer blur moved against his field of vision as the fingers were withdrawn; and then a white smear that might be a face hovered above him.

"Hermione Brannigan," came the soft answer.

It was the girl. Raider uttered another sigh as he tugged against the ropes, trying to make a bit of slack. That bastard Colby knew what he was doing.

"Can you loosen these ropes?"

"I dasn't!" she said, frightened. "If'n I do, they'll know, mister."

Shit. Raider squeezed his eyes shut tight, his head pounding with the granddaddy of all headaches. There wasn't a part of his body that didn't ache. When he opened them again, his vision had adjusted to the darkness. The girl was no longer a blur; her face was white above a gray dress.

"Water," he said, touching his tongue to his lips. "Please!"

"I brung it."

Hermione turned away for a minute and then came back to sit on the edge of the bed, holding up his head while she brought a tin dipper to his lips. The water was sharply cold. Some slopped over, wetting his cheeks and running down his neck into his shirt, staining the bare mattress.

Raider resisted the impulse to suck greedily. He wet his mouth and again ran his tongue over his lips before he let any of the water trickle down into his belly. It gathered in the center of his gut like an ice cake.

"Ahhhh!" His voice was no longer a croak as he finished what was in the dipper and sighed. "More, please."

"Shush!" said the girl. "Hold yer voice down, mister. They's all asleep, them's in the house, but they c'n wake up awful sudden-like. That's enough water fer now, I'll give you some more later."

There was a drawl to this girl's words that carried the mark of the Border States. Missouri, maybe. Raider uttered another low sigh and tried to flex his fingers. The ropes sawing into his wrists had cut off the circulation in his hands, and now he realized that his extremities were icy.

"You got to loosen the ropes," he said anxiously. "I can't feel anything in my hands and my feet. Blood poisoning will set in if you don't."

Hermione scowled and turned her head, listening to the sounds of the house. Raider stopped breathing for a minute, until the roar of blood rushing past his inner ears stilled. He picked up a chorus of low snores coming from another part of the house. He decided there were two snorers, working in counterpoint.

"You've done this much," he said. "You can loosen the ropes. Please!"

Hermione knotted her brow, studying him closely. She was younger than he had first thought downstairs —no more than a child, although as big as her mother. Her size and her work-lined face had fooled him.

"You promise you won't try to escape?"

Raider managed a wan smile, wondering how long it would take him to recover use of his hands and his feet. He had a sudden image of himself belly-flopping across the floor of the room, dragging himself along on his elbows, bouncing down the flight of stairs—

He shook his head to get rid of the picture. "Honey," he said, "I won't be goin' anywhere for quite awhile, unless someone carries me."

She touched his hand, felt how cold he was, and bit on her lip. "All right, I'll do it. But I cain't loosen them very much, or they'll know fer sure."

"Thank you," said Raider. "You're an angel of mercy, sent from heaven."

But before she touched the ropes, Hermione backed up a pace and then turned and went to the curtainless window. She looked out toward the barn and the corral. Raider saw she was barefoot, as she had been downstairs; but apparently she had slipped into her dress and nothing else. The dress was shapeless, but in profile, her small breasts jutted.

"Somebody on guard?"

"Mabbottson's up in the barn loft," said Hermione. Satisfied, she came back to the bed. "He c'n see back into the canyon an' toward the road, both."

She bent over his wrist and began to tug at the knot, tongue soon slipping out of the corner of her mouth as she worked against the hard rawhide. It would have been easier with a light, but Hermione stuck to it, sucking in disgustedly several times. There was nothing Raider could do except turn his wrist toward her.

"Anybody else?" he said, gasping when she unwittingly brought pressure on the rope. "On guard?"

"Hinckley's out front, by the gate. 'Cept he's probably sleepin'. Even Bartlett says he ain't worth a rat's asshole fer anything more'n a good fart."

The crudity startled Raider; it reminded him of Amity. At least Hermione didn't seem interested in making him prove he was a man.

"Why do they keep Hinckley in the gang?"

"He drives the stage. Hol' still!"

Suddenly the rope loosened, and Raider bit down on his lower lip to swallow a scream. Ten thousand needles were stabbing into his arm from fingertips to shoulder. The agony showed on his face, and sweat poured over his forehead. Hermione saw the sheen as she worked the rope out of the deep burn mark.

"Hol' on," she said kindly. "The misery will let up in a minute er so."

She did not remove the rope from his wrist, and Raider instinctively tightened, afraid she was about to retie the knot. But Hermione moved around to the other side of the bed. That knot proved even trickier. It took almost twice as long as the first, but at last she sighed in satisfaction and sat back, eying Raider as he swallowed a moan.

His right arm seemed numb. After a minute, the needles stopped jabbing into his left arm. He flexed both sets of fingers, working them until they stopped feeling like fat, lifeless sausages.

"Thank you," he said. "Maybe someday I can do you a favor, Hermione. How about my feet?"

"No more!" she said. "Not now. Look, if'n you promise me somethin' cross-your-heart-an'-hope-to-die, I'll help you escape."

"What promise do you want me to make?"

"That you take me with you when you go!"

Raider sighed; he had expected the request. "How old are you, Hermione?"

"Fifteen," she admitted reluctantly. "But I'm strong as a horse an' I c'n work all day 'thout gittin' tired!"

"Brannigan your pa?"

There was hatred in her voice as she acknowledged the fact. "He beats me, an' he beats Ma, too. When he gits likkered up, he's liable to do anythin'—he broke Maw's arm, oncet, cracked up her ribs a couple times."

"Anybody else in your family? Relatives who could take you in—any brothers?"

"I guess Maw's got fambly, back East some'eres. I don' even know what town, er what state. My brother Tim tuck off three year ago, when he got enough growth on't him t' stand up t' Pa. He promised then t' come back fer me, but I don' think he's ever gonna come."

"How old is Tim?"

"He was jes' fourteen when he tuck off."

Raider sighed again. Movement had returned to his hands, although they still hurt plenty. He tested the ropes that held his ankles, inching down a bit at the same time.

"Who's snoring?"

"Pa," said Hermione. "An' Billy Bartlett. Maw, too, but they's out-snorin' her."

"Where are the rest?"

"In the bunkhouse, 'cept Mabbottson an' Hinckley."

"What time is it?"

"Jes' past eleven. Pa an' Bartlett got likkered up until they had t' help each other up t' bed, 'bout an hour ago. We ain't gotta worry about them."

Eleven. Mulligan hadn't had time to ride to Coffin Canyon and back. Too bad Doc was no longer staying in the big house. Time was running out.

"You know what your pa is mixed up in?"

"Robbin' the silver shipments," said Hermione matter-of-factly. "Most of what they stole is buried down in th' old root cellar."

"I'm working for the Coffin Queen," said Raider. "I'm a Pinkerton agent."

"I figgered you were some kinda law, th' way Pa near shit his britches."

Raider managed a smile, although he was not yet ready to laugh. He tested the loose ropes and lifted one shoulder a fraction of an inch and then the other. If his feet weren't tied, he thought he could move.

"What time does the guard change?"

"Bartlett tol' them ever' two hour. I don' know who's comin' on next—they was gonna draw straws when they got t' the bunkhouse."

"At midnight, then."

"I guess. Hinckley come out right after pa an' Bartlett went up t' bed."

Less than an hour. Raider's mind whirled with schemes. The girl was the problem. He didn't want to be burdened with Hermione, yet he had to convince her of the importance of helping him escape right now. It would take him at least ten minutes to regain full use of his legs.

"Hermione, if I promise to come back for you—"

"No way, mister!" she said, cutting him off. "You think I'm jest a kid, but I c'n ride all day. You take me with you, or you ain't goin'!"

Raider surrendered to the inevitable. "All right, you've got a deal. But it's got to be right now, while Hinckley is still on guard. Do you know what they did with my horse?"

"Put him in the corral. Yer saddle's in the barn."

Raider tried to remember whether anyone had picked up his gun. Someone must have, but there was no telling where it might be now. Probably in the bunkhouse.

"Any guns downstairs?"

"Pa's shotgun. He keeps his rifle an' handgun locked up in a cupboard."

"The one in the kitchen?"

When Hermione nodded, Raider knew a measure of

relief. He hadn't paid much attention to the cupboard, but it was something a two-year-old kid could pop with a penknife.

"You really want to go with me?"

"Mister, I ain't riskin' Pa turnin' me over to those bastards fer the fun of it!"

The thought disgusted Raider. He vowed to kill Brannigan if the chance came his way.

"Cut me loose," he said.

Hermione did just that. She produced a knife from someplace in her skirts and began to saw at the knots while Raider tugged his hands out of the other ropes. It was almost a minute before the last bond parted, and then the girl had to help him roll painfully to the edge of the bed and sit up.

"Jesus!" he said softly; it was as much a prayer as a curse. It was almost five minutes before he dared test his strength, holding to Hermione while standing. His knees wanted to buckle, but he managed a dragging step and then another. He made it as far as the wall, putting out his hands to support himself on stiffened arms. His head hung down between his shoulders as he did breathing exercises.

"Go get what you need from your room," he said. "I'll be ready when you get back."

Hermione slipped out and was back in less than two minutes. She carried a bundle wrapped in a skirt and had a pair of shoes tied together around her neck. He leaned on the girl as they made their way down the stairs, Raider wishing he had pulled off his boots. Three times they stopped dead as risers creaked, but the sound of the snoring, louder in the hall, did not alter.

They made the kitchen without trouble, and there Raider borrowed Hermione's knife to pop the lock on the cupboard. The girl lit the stub of a candle, shielding it while he drew out the Winchester and a Colt Peacemaker. Brannigan's gun belt was far too big for him, but he spotted his own hanging on a chair, along with his hat.

He tested one of his own cartridges in the Winchester, relieved to find that it was rifled for a .44. The Colt was a .45. He hurriedly transferred bullets from Brannigan's belt to empty slots in his own and then started for the door.

"Can both guards see the kitchen?" he asked.

Hermione shook her head as she snuffed the candle flame. "Jest Hinckley." And she pointed out the gate to answer Raider's next question.

A mantel clock chimed the quarter hour. It was 11:45; later than the girl had said. In fifteen minutes, the guard would change. Raider arched his back to test his reflexes; he still ached, but there was nothing to be done for that.

"Stay here!" he said in a sharp whisper as Hermione started to follow him outside. "I'll come back for you."

The girl swallowed a protest as Raider slipped out and moved across the porch, staying in the shadows of the house wall. The sky was bright with a million stars, but there was no moon; the feeble crescent had dipped over the Sierras. He got his bearings on the gate, and on an old live oak that Hermione had said sheltered Hinckley.

Raider dropped from the porch, landing in some kind of muck that splattered up onto his trousers. He made a face and froze for another twenty seconds. The sound hadn't carried to Hinckley. He crouched and ran toward the tree. Halfway there, the shadows shifted slightly. He realized that Hinckley was seated on a bench that circled the tree.

The man was still asleep. Raider used the Colt to make that sleep last longer and stretched Hinckley out on the ground. He drew the bandit's gun and stuck it in his own belt; then he took his Winchester as well.

Burdened, he decided to leave both rifles with Hermione. He started to step away from the tree—

"Hinckley! Come on, you bastard, wake up!"

Another man had appeared, rifle under his arm. He came across the yard, heading straight for Raider.

—

CHAPTER TWENTY-FIVE

Raider felt his heart sink as he melted back into the shadows of the tree.

"Hinckley! You sonofabitch, if I tell Billy you was sleepin' on guard, he'll have yer balls for breakfast! Wake up, you no-good shithead!"

Raider moved back farther and trod on Hinckley's body. He almost went sprawling but caught himself just in time, stepping up onto the bench, nearly banging his head on one of the branches. He wondered whether the man coming were Mabbottson or the relief. Whoever, the clock in the kitchen had to be off.

He leaned the excess Winchester against the trunk of the tree, testing to make sure it wouldn't fall over. Then he took the barrel of the other rifle into both hands. The other man was only paces away, but he showed no sign of stopping.

"Hinckley—"

Raider swung the rifle with all of his strength. The butt smashed into the man's face, crushing cartilage in his nose. His hands went up, and he stumbled backward and went down with a strangled cry. Before he could make another noise, Raider jumped down from the bench and kicked him in the temple.

The man didn't move. Raider knelt, listening; he wasn't breathing. He got up, brushing off his knees, and checked Hinckley again. The latter breathed easily.

The stock of the Winchester he had used as a club was cracked. Raider left it on the ground, grabbing the other to make a run toward the house. Hermione was waiting for him; she came out onto the porch, stumbling in her fright.

"Did you kill them both?" she cried softly.

"Was that second one Mabbottson?" asked Raider, parrying the girl's question.

"Yes. Hurry, 'fore the others rouse out. You made enough noise t' wake the dead."

Raider hurried with the girl to the barn. Slipping through the little door, he struck a match and lit the lantern. He hung it on a post while he started searching for his saddle. He found it at last, and to his surprise, he also found his Remington, kicked aside in the dust and old straw covering the floor. He took a few seconds to break the gun open and blow the dust out of the action, and then he reloaded it. He gave Hermione the Peacemaker.

"Do you know how to use this?"

"I c'n pull the trigger. Last time I tried, it knocked me on my ass. But that was before Tim tuck off."

"Don't pull the trigger unless you absolutely have to. And for Christ's sake, not while you're behind me! Now which one of these saddles do you use?"

"I usual ride bareback," said Hermione. "I guess any will do."

"Oh, great!" said Raider, groaning. "You said you can ride all day."

"I can, bareback!"

He chose the lightest saddle he could find and told Hermione to pick up two sets of blankets. The girl also took the rifle as Raider staggered out of the barn, burdened by the two saddles. The horses woke as he slipped the rails on the corral gate, his own coming over to welcome him. Hermione caught another that settled as she stroked its muzzle, and then she brought it over to Raider.

Raider hurried, but he was still half-crippled from being tied to the bed. It was at least five minutes before the two of them swung into the saddle, just as the bunkhouse door opened, spilling light. A man stepped out, running his fingers through his hair. He saw the pair of riders come out of the corral as another man came out behind him, carrying a rifle.

"Hey! Who the hell is that?" cried the first man, startled. "Colby!"

Raider cursed silently as he kneed the horse. Just as he had feared, the next shift had been awakened by an alarm clock.

"Come on, girl!" he hissed. "Get the hell out of here!"

Hermione followed his lead. The two horses broke into a run, heading straight toward the men in the bunkhouse. At the last minute Raider veered away, the girl on his tail, and headed for the gate, his original destination. He wasn't exactly sure of his present location but he wasn't about to risk that trail back through the canyon and over the back side of the mountain on a moonless night.

"It's the Pinkerton!" cried Colby, outraged. "And Brannigan's brat! Get them!"

Colby fired his rifle, and Raider felt the wind of the slug pass by his ear. Several more shots followed quickly as the first man came to his senses and drew his gun, and bedlam broke out as others tumbled out of the bunkhouse in their drawers. Raider and the girl clung to the necks of their mounts to make themselves as small as possible as they rode out of the yard beneath the arched sign of the gate.

"Where does this road take us?" he yelled.

"Carson City!" answered Hermione. "Once you pass Blasted Rock! Turn left there, an' it's the Gap road up t' Coffin Canyon!"

"How far is Blasted Rock?"

"Five mile!"

Raider cast a look back. As yet, pursuit had not been organized, but it was only a matter of minutes before the gang would be hot on their tails. If they rode on to

Carson City, he could send Doc an urgent telegram, warning him what action to take. Slap Helena Coffin into one of Marshal Seth Morgan's jail cells. Alert Junius and his brothers to take that damn dynamite out of the mine. They should have removed the stuff as soon as they discovered it.

But even as he formulated the scheme, Raider knew he was going to ride straight back to Coffin Canyon. Any plans Bartlett had hatched with Helena would be moved up to right now, and there might not be time to send a warning.

Half a mile passed beneath the flying hooves while Raider reached his decision. Hermione clung to the neck of her horse, but as he eyed her, he saw that she was in control and able to keep up. The ranch was a good two miles back now. He hoped the horses were rested enough to go full out until they reached Blasted Rock.

Five minutes later they reached the junction and reined up. Raider patted his horse on the neck while the animals blew for a moment, massive chests heaving; then he slipped down and walked back fifty feet, listening for sounds of pursuit. They couldn't have more than five minutes' lead.

"I'm going up the mountain," he said, coming back to swing into the saddle. "You head for Carson City."

"No!" cried Hermione. "You promised to take me with you! I'm comin'!"

"Don't be a damn fool! We gotta split up, make it harder for them to follow us. Besides, I promised to help you get away—I didn't say I'd take care of you for the rest of my life."

"I'm comin'," the girl said stubbornly.

Shit! Double shit! Precious seconds were slipping away. "How far is Graveyard Gap?"

"Fast horse, mebbe two hours."

"All right, come on."

Hermione smiled as she swung out after Raider

around Blasted Rock, which had been struck once by a super lightning bolt that had left it fragmented. If she had known he was planning to leave her with Zach and Amity, the smile would have turned to a scowl.

He stayed alert as they retraced Doc's path when he came down the mountain, unaware that back at the ranch, Billy Bartlett had been roused from a drunken stupor by Colby and Jack. It had taken fifteen minutes to get him down to the kitchen, during which time no one had had the presence of mind to go after them.

"Assholes!" roared Bartlett. "Sweet merciful mother of Jesus, why did you stick me with such shit-for-brains morons! Goddamn it, you'll never catch them now!"

"I wanted to go after them," said Jack sullenly. "These bastards wouldn't help me, Billy."

The hapless Hinckley had been brought into the kitchen, where he sat nursing a large lump on his head. Bartlett glowered at him and then walked over and backhanded him. Hinckley cringed away, sniveling as he wiped blood from his nose on the sleeve of his shirt.

"I oughta shoot you where you sit!" muttered Bartlett. And then he turned his anger on Brannigan. "It's your fault, goddamn it—that goddamn brat of yours cut him loose."

"What do we do now?" asked Colby.

"I gotta think," said Billy, pressing the heels of his hands to his temples. "Shit!"

"Why don't we call it quits?" asked Brannigan nervously. "We got enough silver, Billy. I say split it up now, fergit that crazy woman."

Bartlett skewered him with a glare. "No, Brannigan," he said softly. "We ain't gonna fergit Helena. All my life I been waitin' fer this one chance, and now that it's been dropped into my lap, I ain't gonna blow it! What we got now is shit compared to what's waitin' once Helena gits control of the mine. There's millions in it, and I intend to have my share!"

Brannigan scuttled back. "Fergit I said anything, Billy. I'm sorry."

"That's the trouble with all you assholes!" said Bartlett. "You're a sorry goddamn lot of fuck-ups! I rue the day I ever laid eyes on the first of you."

"What are we gonna do?" asked Jack, after it was clear Bartlett had finished. Billy sighed.

"The only goddamn thing we can do. I can't wait fer Mulligan to git back—mount up. We're ridin' fer Coffin Canyon."

CHAPTER TWENTY-SIX

Raider pushed the horses until the grade gradually became steeper. Then he turned in his saddle to look back, wishing for a moon, to show the road below. They moved through shadows that suddenly became impenetrable as a rock outcropping or a clump of trees loomed overhead.

Raider cast a glance at the girl and thought he saw her mount misstep, almost breaking the gait. He reined up and fell back beside her, but the animal came on easily.

"You okay?" he asked.

"Yeah," said Hermione, looking back. "I am now."

Raider chalked it up to imagination and poor light. They were alone in a night world that was empty except for the bare jutting mountains, stark black trees that suddenly skewered the sky, and an upside down bowl of bright, glittering stars. Around them was silence, except for the clip-clop of their horses over rocky stretches of the road and the animals' occasional blowing. Ahead, the road was a gray ribbon that now snaked out of sight around the bulge of the mountain, now appeared above the tree line overhead. But it was everrising, as though the men who built in this Godforsaken outland had sought to construct a highway that would take them to heaven.

Black and gray and silver: it might have been a world of the dead. And then an owl swooped low, its wings battering the air just over Raider's head and startling his horse.

Hermione jumped. "What was that?"

"Just an owl," said Raider, although his own heart was beating faster. "That's all."

"Yeah," said the girl sheepishly.

They rode on, rising steadily from the flats, until half an hour later Raider heard her curse.

"Shit. Wait up—my horse just went lame."

The animal half-danced along, one foreleg held up to paw the air. Raider stopped, swung down from the saddle, and caught the reins of the other animal.

"Whoa, fella," he said. "Easy, now, hold on."

"What is it?" asked Hermione anxiously as he caught the hoof, struck a match, and cursed himself.

"Split hoof." He lowered the leg. "Get down. You ain't goin' any farther with this horse."

"Shit! Sonofabitch!"

Hermione cursed steadily if unimaginatively as she dismounted, half sliding down the horse's flank. She took a look at the damage for herself as Raider struck another match.

"That tears it!" she said. "Now what are we gonna do?"

"The sensible thing is to find some water and some grass and bed down. But I ain't got time to be sensible. And I'm not carryin' you double to Coffin Canyon."

"I'll walk, then!" she said hotly. "I still got a gun. I c'n take care of myself."

"You're still wet behind the ears," said Raider, half in amusement and half in disgust. Shit! The things he let himself in for.

He checked the road down. "I don't think there's anybody following us. How far you figger to Graveyard Gap?"

"I guess another hour, from what Pa says. I ain't never been up this way—ain't never been noplace since we came to the ranch, 'cept a couple of the neighbors'."

"That's wonderful!" said Raider. "Now just what in sweet hell am I supposed to do with you?"

"You ain't gotta do nothin'! Just go on, go on about

yer business. I got along 'fore you came, I c'n git along now."

"That's why you begged me to help you escape."

"Seems to me you was the one doin' the beggin'."

Raider threw up his hands. "All right. I owe you. I'll get you up to Coffin Canyon, or some other place within reason. But you can't stay with me, you know."

"I didn't figger I could," she said quietly.

He went on without acknowledging her words. "Hell, I don't even have a home—I'm always on the trail, ridin' from one case to another. Once this case is wrapped up, I'm just liable to be sent to Montana, or Texas, or anyplace else from Timbuktu to South America."

"What's Timbuktu?"

"I don't really know," he admitted. "Someplace way the hell and gone far off, maybe in Asia. The end of the world. The point is, girl, I travel fast and I travel light. I can't take you with me, and I can't be responsible for what happens to you after we separate."

"I'll find somethin'."

"Yeah, well, what you oughta do is find yourself a good-size town, maybe Carson City, maybe cross the mountains to Sacramento or San Francisco. There's always jobs for a willin' worker, and there's always men lookin' for a wife. You're a pretty girl, Hermione—at least, you would be, if you washed your face and brushed your hair and had a decent dress."

His words embarrassed the girl. She shrugged away and said without looking at him, "Are we gonna stand here talkin' all night, or are we gonna ride?"

"Get up," said Raider, swinging back into the saddle and offering her his hand. "Come on, dammit! I ain't takin' you all the way to Coffin tonight—you'll slow me down too much. I'm gonna leave you with some people I know who have a place in the canyon below Graveyard Gap. An old prospector and his granddaughter. You'll be safe there."

Hermione swung aboard easily and settled behind Raider, her arms about his waist. Neither one of them said anything as he urged the horse forward; their words seemed to have dried up. After perhaps fifteen minutes, she squirmed around a bit and let her face fall against his back and her hands across his thighs. She dozed, hardly a weight against him, holding to him in trust. The black horse moved on, carrying the extra burden without protest.

She was only a kid. Fifteen, and never been anyplace, didn't know anything except grueling work for all of her days. Hell, she probably hadn't known ten people in the world until the gang rode into Brannigan's ranch.

Raider knew she was only a child; but he was also aware of the small breasts pressing against his back, the trusting fingers only an inch away from his cock. The night had cooled considerably; the sweat had dried on his face. But his ears still burned for what he was thinking. . . .

Dawn tinged the eastern sky as Raider rode into Coffin Canyon, alone. In the time it took for him to ride through the town, the sky's blush grew from a maiden's promise to long, stretching fingers of pink; and then the bright rim of the sun touched the distant horizon, almost blindingly, so sudden was the change.

Coffin Canyon was dead quiet, the main street shadowed by its structures so that it remained gray. Raider spotted the sun between buildings, but it wasn't up far enough to do more than briefly expose the colors surrounding him. A poster in a saloon window on the west side of the street was bright red for an instant, and then a colorless blur again.

Raider had dropped Hermione off with Zach and Amity, after making his way down a precarious trail below the Gap. The old prospector had been outraged at being awakened in the middle of the night; but when Amity realized who their visitor was, she had come to Raider and welcomed him with a hug and a kiss.

"I was hopin' you'd come back, John O'Toole!"

"I brought someone to stay you with for a couple of days," Raider had said. Hermione waited just outside the door of the cabin. "Some company for you."

"Yer the only company I want."

Amity was sullen when Raider first brought Hermione into the cabin, until she realized that she was only a child. She welcomed her then, while Raider passed a few words with Zach, bringing him up to date on everything that had happened.

"You better stay away from the Queen for a while, Zach. Maybe for good. Once this is over, they'll find that new vein you uncovered."

"Hell, O'Toole, I ain't been near the Queen since the day I showed you the dynamite. I ain't no danged fool! You want me to take you up the canyons again?"

"Not without a moon. I'll stay with the road."

The Coffin houses, the big house and the three that belonged to the sons, were dark as Raider rode into the yard of the mine. The office showed a single dim light; then a man stepped out of the shadows of the porch, working the lever of his Winchester.

"Hold it right there, mister!"

"Is that you, Sawyer?"

The man relaxed. "Yeah, O'Toole. Where you been? Junius was raisin' holy hell last night 'cause you wasn't here."

"Did something happen?"

"Naw, just the yellin'." He turned and spat a stream of tobacco juice. "I guess once this guardin' job is over, I'll move on. I've had about all of them Coffins I can take."

"I know what you mean. They're pretty hard to take, the lot of them. Have you seen Doc Weatherbee?"

"The snake-oil salesman? Not that I recollect, not the last day or so."

Shit. Raider wanted to tell Doc everything that had happened before he faced Junius. He wondered if Doc had returned from his errand of the day before. It would be just like the bastard to miss the wrap-up of the case. But of course, that would mean more credit to himself.

"Stay loose," said Raider. "If you see any strangers, stop them and hold them. And pass the word to the others."

"Sure." Sawyer spat again, and Raider turned back and rode out of the yard.

The shadows were stretching, becoming tenuous as the sky overhead lightened. He could see easily now as he turned into Abernathy's livery and dismounted, letting the horse drink from the watering trough while he entered the barn. He spotted the Studebaker and rapped on the board side.

"Doc? You in there?"

No answer. Raider struck a match and used it to locate a lantern, and he struck a second to light the wick. Climbing onto the box, he held the light inside. Everything was neat and in its proper place; Doc's bedroll was stowed out of sight.

He hadn't slept here the night before. Raider climbed down again, wondering whether to wake up Junius and give him his report or to wait a while and try to locate Doc. A cock crowed; the town was coming to life. Raider left the barn as the crow was answered from another part of town, and a tree behind Constantine Abernathy's house suddenly came alive with bird song as a roosting flock woke.

Raider removed his hat and scratched his head as daylight broke over the town. He was tired despite the few snatched hours of sleep tied to Brannigan's bed. The all-night ride had taken a lot out of him.

The idea of sleep was almost too appealing to resist. He yawned widely, cracking his jaw, and caught the reins to lead the horse toward Junius' house. The information he carried couldn't wait.

The street was empty, but some of the houses showed lights. Somewhere, a door slammed, and a woman yelled at a kid who had failed to keep the woodbox full. The big house was dark, but there were lights in the front and the back of Junius Coffin's place.

Raider tied the horse to the hitching post and went around to the back to find Junius' wife and the hired girl starting breakfast in the kitchen.

"Good morning," he said, tipping his hat. "Sorry to be comin' by so early, Miz Coffin, but I need to see your husband right away."

"You're the second visitor this morning," said Mrs. Coffin, dusting flour from her hands. She was a substantial woman in her early forties who spoke with a faint German accent. "Mr. Coffin and his brothers are in the parlor."

All three Coffins had dressed hastily. Raider knocked on the sliding doors and opened them without waiting for an invitation. Junius spun around.

"Where the hell have you been?" he demanded.

"Learnin' things," said Raider. "For instance, the name of the person behind all your troubles."

"Helena," said Jasper. "We already know."

That shook Raider a mite, but he tried not to show it as he revealed what had happened to him after following Helena. The three brothers listened intently until he finished.

"The silver is at Brannigan's ranch. Get up a posse an' we can get it back today."

"We don't have time to do that," said Junius sourly. "Nor are Helena's henchmen going to wait to start action. Read this."

He handed across a crumpled note written on soiled foolscap. Printed, rather; in unsteady block letters, the note read:

SELL THE QUEEN BY THREE O'CLOCK
THIS AFTERNOON, OR YOU WON'T HAVE
NOTHING TO SELL.

"This was brought in about half an hour ago," said
Junius.

"Describe the man who brought it."

He did so. Raider heard him out, nodding. "That's
the one they call Jack. The gang must have headed up
the back side of the mountain while I was comin' up
the Gap road."

"You better read this, too," said Junius, giving him
the report on Helena. "Weatherbee got this about noon
yesterday." Neither he nor Raider knew Doc had
carried the report around overnight before he had
gotten around to decoding it. If Raider had known, he
and Doc would have come perilously close to mixing it
up again.

He scanned the report. "A busy woman," he said.
"With what I learned at Brannigan's, there's enough to
send Helena to the gallows."

He glanced at the brothers in turn, looking for a
reaction that might say whether one of the trio was involved with Helena in her scheme. Junius and Jasper
had been doing all of the talking. Jonathan toyed with
his coffee, stirring it constantly. He looked like death
warmed over, a three-day stubble on his cheeks. From
time to time he winced in pain from his hangover.

"We were just going to send for Weatherbee," said
Junius. "We need a council of war. It might be better
if you go."

"Where's he stayin'?"

"He moved back into the big house. Gave the woman
some kind of cock-and-bull story."

"All right. I'll be right back."

Raider tipped the brim of his hat as he walked
through the kitchen again. He didn't bother with the
horse. No lights showed yet in CeeCee's house, and he

banged on the front door for nearly five minutes before
Maureen appeared, clutching an old wrapper about her.
She studied Raider through a crack in the door.

"Tell Doc Weatherbee John O'Toole wants him."

"He ain't here," said the girl nervously. "He went
away yest'day."

"Went away where?" said Raider, scowling.

"I dunno, mister. He's gone, that's all."

"That's damn funny. His wagon is in the livery."

"I tol' you, I don' know, mister!"

The girl was on the edge of hysteria. She tried to
close the door. Raider reached out to stop her but then
shook his head and turned away. Now where the hell
had Doc gone? He started down the steps.

"You, there!"

Raider stopped on the bottom step in surprise. Cee-
Cee Coffin peered around the corner of the house,
beckoning to him frantically.

"Yes, you! Come here!"

Tufts of hair stood up all over CeeCee's head, and
one suspender hung half down his arm. He wore carpet
slippers but no shirt.

"You're Weatherbee's partner. The other Pinkerton."

Raider blinked in further surprise. "I am," he said.
"Do you know where Doc went?"

"Helena locked him in the attic."

CHAPTER TWENTY-SEVEN

CeeCee kept peering around, as though expecting someone to come up on him. Raider tried to assimilate the shock of what the old man was saying as he pulled the story out.

"She promised to help me get the mine back, but she wants all the silver for herself! Greedy, that's what she is. No better'n Junius. She's makin' the boys sell out. You better help your partner, mister, before Helena kills him."

"Slow down!" said Raider. "Backtrack there a jump or two, old-timer. You say Helena's got Doc locked up in the attic? What happened?"

"She's had her whelps watching the house," said CeeCee, going off at a tangent. Doc had described him as crazy as a hoot owl, but except for his tendency to ramble, right now he seemed rational to Raider.

"I been up all night," the old man continued, "waitin' for the chance to sneak out. Figgered I'd get Seth Morgan. About time he did somethin' to earn his salary. She'll kill me, too, just as soon as she thinks it's safe. But I fooled her!"

"Get back to Doc," said Raider.

"I told you!" said CeeCee, frustrated by Raider's refusal to understand. "His life ain't worth a plugged nickel unless you get him out right now. They're up there in Helena's room right now, her'n that hardcase, plottin' out what they're gonna do."

"Bartlett?"

"I don't know his name, an' I don't give a damn," said CeeCee. "Jonathan's the only one worth a hoot.

Tricked me into signin' over my mine, my own sons! Him an' Jasper! How d'ya like that fer a fine how-d'ya-do?"

"Is Jonathan involved in this?"

"No, no! You ain't listenin'! You gonna do somethin', or are you gonna wait 'till yer partner is pushin' up daisies? Ya danged fool!"

Raider stared up at the blank windows of the house, musing.

"Which is Helena's room?"

"Right over yer head."

Even though they had been whispering, Raider worried that they might have been heard. He grabbed CeeCee's arm and moved him along the side of the house until they reached the back corner.

"How many people in the house?" he asked.

"Helena and her whelps. The hired girl. Yancy, the hired man, has a room over the stable." CeeCee counted on his fingers. "An' the hardcase. That's all."

Four women and one man. Of course, Helena was as deadly as any man. The girls, Zelzah and Moravia, were an unknown quantity. The hired girl could be dismissed.

"You said the girls were watching the house. Where are they now?"

"Gone to bed when that man came. Hussies!"

Raider wondered briefly what CeeCee would say if he knew about Helena's career. His own tiredness had vanished now that he was in a pressure situation. His brain spun furiously, discarding one scheme after another.

"I'm going to get Junius."

"Ain't time for that!" said CeeCee, catching Raider's arm. "I heard Helena say they was gonna kill him before that man left."

"Christ! How do you get to the attic?"

"Up the back stairs, off the kitchen," said CeeCee. "But Helena locked the door. She's carryin' the key."

Given time, Raider knew he could pick the lock; but his pocketknife, with a built-in lockpick, had been taken from him at Brannigan's. He stepped away from the corner of the house, craning his neck to look up. There was a single window high under the eaves; it seemed impossibly far away.

If Doc could drop him a rope, he could go up hand-over-hand and get in that way, but Doc didn't even know he was down here. And Helena wasn't stupid enough to leave him untied.

"I got no choice," he said, half to himself. "I gotta go through the house."

Mind made up, Raider moved around to the back steps. Time was passing, and he had already wasted too many precious seconds and minutes. But he stopped to sit down and tug off his boots. He was going to have to move as quietly as possible once through the door.

CeeCee clung to the corner with both hands, watching nervously as Raider placed his boots beside the steps and started up. Dew wet the steps and the porch; his socks were soaked through by the time he reached the back door. CeeCee had left it unlocked when he came out, and Raider slipped through, easing it shut behind him.

The small kitchen was dominated by a Kalamazoo range and a couple of work tables. A wet sink with a pump was across from the stove, beneath the windows. Raider checked a swinging door: it led to the pantry. Another gave onto the dining room. A door with a latch was the only other possibility, but when he opened it, he saw it led down, into the cellar.

Cursing CeeCee for not being more specific with his directions, Raider started toward the dining room—and saw through the glass bull's-eye Moravia approaching. The back door was too far away, and she would see him jumping from the porch. The only other choice was the pantry. He ducked through and used his fingertips to stop the quivering of the swinging door.

He heard Moravia yawn and then sigh as he looked around and spotted another latched door in the corner. That must be the back stairs. But before he could reach it, the girl came into the pantry.

"Oh!" She stared in shock as Raider spun on her. "John O'Toole! What are you doing here?"

Raider blinked. "You don't know?"

Moravia smiled. She cocked her hip, bringing her breasts into prominence as she stroked one thigh. Now he saw that her nightgown was nearly transparent.

"No," she said, her voice dropping several decibels. "But I hope you came to see me. If you're real quiet, I can slip you into my bedroom."

She showed the tip of her tongue between her teeth. Christ, was that all these women had in their heads?

Raider moved closer to the girl and took her upper arms into his hands. Moravia was as desirable as any girl he had ever seen, and the adrenalin that was already in his blood could merely take a detour to affect a different part of his body. Her lips opened, ready for a kiss—

"What about Doc?"

"What?" Startled by his question, she shook her head. "You mean Dr. Weatherbee? What about him?"

"I came to get him," said Raider. "Before your mother decides to slit his throat."

Moravia tried to twist free, but Raider tightened his grip on her arms. Her face flamed in anger.

"I don't know what you're talking about! How dare you say such a thing about my mother?"

"It's the truth, isn't it? Or don't you know about all those houses your mother ran?"

Moravia stiffened, and then she went limp and sagged against him. For a minute he thought she was going to faint. But she recovered and shook her head bitterly.

"She said you were a Pinkerton. I suppose it's all over—now we'll have to pack up and move on again.

God, I'm getting so sick of jumping from town to town, staying one jump ahead of the law!"

"Now, you listen, and listen good," said Raider sharply. "I know Bartlett or one of those others is with your mother right now. You've been watchin' the house for her."

"I don't know what you're talking about!" said Moravia hotly. "Watching the house for what?"

"You sayin' you haven't been up all night?"

"No, I have not. At least, not all night," she amended. "What have you been doing—spying on me?"

"CeeCee saw you prowlin'."

"Him!" Moravia's tone was filled with derision. "Crazy old man! I told Mother this was one time her scheme wouldn't work, but she wouldn't listen."

"Were you up or not?" demanded Raider.

"I was, for a little while. I . . . met a feller," she said. "What's it to you, John O'Toole? Just because we have a swim together doesn't give you proprietary rights to my body."

"What about Doc?"

"What about him? I suppose he's in bed—that's where he was heading the last time I saw him."

"CeeCee says Helena locked him in the attic."

"He's crazy! Why would she do that?"

"Listen, don't you understand?" Raider demanded impatiently. "She told you we're Pinkertons, right? The scheme is up! We got a report on Helena that goes all the way back to Philadelphia. She ain't missed many stops in between."

"Please, let go of me," said Moravia. When Raider complied, she sighed and looked away, but she made no effort to get away from him. "She said this would be the last time, that this time we'd be fixed for life. She said we'd go to Europe and find a duke or a count or something for Zelzah and me. I believed her. I always believe her."

Suddenly she spun on Raider. "Believe me, John

O'Toole, I get so damned tired of living a lie! But what are we supposed to do? She is our mother."

Raider decided she was telling the truth. "You know Helena's behind the silver robberies? That she's plannin' to get control of the Queen for herself?"

"No." Moravia shook her head. "I don't know any of that. She never tells us anything."

It was possible. Helena could want to keep her daughters from knowing what she was about, even if she had caused the deaths of a score of men without blinking an eye. She didn't draw the line at using them for window dressing, however. It was respectable, a widow traveling with two daughters.

"Maybe CeeCee missed the truth about you bein' in on it," he said. "But Doc is still in trouble."

"I tell you, the old man is crazy," said Moravia. "Let me check his room—I'm sure I'll find him sleeping peacefully in his bed."

"All right," said Raider. "But I'm coming with you." And then he added, "The back stairs. I don't want to run into your mother's friend."

Moravia shrugged and led him through the door in the back of the pantry. The stairs were enclosed and made three sharp turns before they came out on a landing in the gloomy back of the second floor. Another door led up, but when Raider tested the latch, it was locked.

Moravia frowned and went down the hall while Raider hung back. She stopped at a door across from her mother's room, rapping lightly. After a minute, she opened it; then she gestured for Raider to join her.

"He was here," she whispered. The bed was unmade, and Doc's possessions were spread across the dresser, his suitcoat hung on the back of the chair.

"He didn't leave half-dressed," said Raider, drawing his gun. "Check the bed, see if it's still warm."

Moravia did as he said. "Cold," she said.

"All right, I'm gonna believe he's in the attic. I just hope he's still alive."

He stepped out of Doc's room, and an instant later, the door across the hall opened, and Billy Bartlett came out. The two men froze in shock; then Bartlett began to claw for his gun, throwing himself aside as Raider fired.

The slug tore through the doorjamb. Raider caught a glimpse of Helena inside the room, staring in disbelief. He dropped to the floor as Bartlett finally drew his weapon and snapped off a shot that went through the space where Raider's head had been half a second earlier.

Raider returned the fire, shooting blind as he crawled along the hall, seeking cover that would let him shoot back. The head of the main stairs was a dozen feet away; he rolled over, firing again, and heard Helena scream.

And then he rolled down the stairs and stopped himself to rise up. Bartlett was still in the bedroom, but Raider could see him in a mirror. For the moment, Bartlett seemed content to stay where he was; Raider used the opportunity to reload his gun.

"My God, what's going on?" Zelzah suddenly appeared in the hall, rubbing sleep grit from her eyes. "What's all the noise?"

Her eyes widened as she saw Raider. "John O'Toole! What on earth—"

Distracted, Raider took his eyes from Bartlett for a moment. The outlaw was using the same mirror to watch him, and now he came rolling into the hall, snapping off three quick shots to make Raider keep his head down. He came to his feet, grabbed Zelzah, and spun her around as a shield.

"Back off, Pink!" he cried. "Or I'll kill the girl!"

"No!" Helena appeared in the door, shaken. "Bartlett, let her go! I order you to let her go!"

"Yer time for orderin' people around is finished,"

said the outlaw. "From now on, you follow orders, Helena! You've fucked up ever'thing, you damn bitch! Move it, Pink, goddamn it! Throw down your gun!"

"I'll remember you, Bartlett," said Raider quietly. "This isn't finished."

"Yer damn right it ain't! The gun!"

Raider pulled his finger away from the trigger and tossed the Remington. It landed eight feet away, halfway between them. Bartlett grinned, a vicious smile that revealed broken and yellowed teeth, and started to lower the barrel of his gun from the hollow of Zelzah's throat. There was no place for Raider to hide. He looked death in the eye—

"No!" Moravia threw something, a small object she had scooped from the dresser: Doc's electric hair brush. It bounced off Bartlett's temple, startling him more than hurting him. He yelled in outrage and let off a shot toward Moravia that broke glass in the room.

She screamed, but Raider had already taken the opportunity to vault the banister as Bartlett snapped off another shot—and his hammer clicked on an empty chamber. The gunman cursed; then he grabbed Zelzah's wrist and dragged her toward the back stairs. Moravia screamed again.

"He's getting away! The back stairs!"

Raider heard her yell the warning, but at the moment he was unable to respond. The shock of landing on the hardwood floor in his stockinged feet slammed through his whole frame, paralyzing him for an instant. Too late, he realized he should have rolled with the landing.

Moravia scooped up Raider's gun and came flying down the stairs to find him leaning against the wall. He sucked air into his lungs, shaking his head when she tried to speak to him, but at last the pain passed, and he could take a tentative step. He was worried that he had broken a bone in his foot.

"Jesus!" he said softly. "Sweet Jesus Christ!"

"They're getting away!" said Moravia again, pressing his gun into his fingers. "Stop him!"

The spirit was willing, but the flesh couldn't obey. Raider heard hoofbeats and looked out the front door to see Bartlett ride out into the street, Zelzah before him in the saddle.

"Damn you!" cried Moravia. "He got away. He took Zelzah!"

"He got away," agreed Raider, "but not for long. We'll get your sister back. Right now, I want to check on Doc."

Limping, he climbed the stairs again. He looked into Helena's room. She was gone. Raider cursed. Nothing was going right.

"Go after your mother. Stop her."

Moravia stared at him for perhaps five seconds and then hurried to do as he said. Raider went back to the attic door and tested it again. Then he threw his shoulder against the panel. New pain stabbed through old wounds, but on the third try, the door broke. He grabbed the edge in both hands and wrenched it free of the latch.

The attic was gloomy, ill-lit by the sunlight that came through dirty dormers. Cobwebs festooned the rafters, and the place was a clutter of junk: broken furniture, trunks for winter clothes, stacks of old magazines and newspapers tied in bundles. A harness hung from overhead, the brass bells on it discolored with age.

"Doc?"

Raider prowled toward the front of the house, peering over obstacles—and found a battered old brass bed shoved under the eaves. Doc lay on the mattress, shrouded in a blanket and trussed from head to foot. A gag was in his mouth, but his eyes burned fire as Raider threw several broken chairs aside to reach him.

"Jesus Christ!" he said. "Can't you stay out of trouble for one goddamn minute?"

What Doc said as Raider removed the gag is better left unrecorded. And what both said when they finally reached the downstairs turned the air blue. CeeCee told them Helena had ridden out in the rig, taking Moravia with her.

CHAPTER TWENTY-EIGHT

"They'll head for Brannigan's and the silver," said Doc after Raider had filled him in on his own adventures. "The scheme to force the boys to sell out is dead."

"I ain't so sure," said Raider. "Bartlett is one mean bastard, Doc. I have a hunch his boys are settin' fuses to that dynamite right now, ready to blow the whole damn side off this mountain."

"Then let's get moving."

Doc had finished dressing, in the clothes he had worn while searching for Raider. For the first time, he strapped on a gun belt and holstered the Diamondback. Raider knew how upset he was at being taken by a woman.

CeeCee was marching up and down the driveway, fretting and fussing as he swished his walking stick against the air, cutting at imaginary enemies.

"Settle down," said Raider. "You ain't the first man to be played for an old fool by Helena. And you ain't married to her. She forgot to shed some earlier husbands before she latched onto you."

"Are there any other back entrances into the mine besides the one in the canyon?" asked Doc as CeeCee stared at them, his eyes bulging.

"There's number four," CeeCee answered. "Down below the opera house. If it ain't collapsed. Been fifteen year since we worked that shaft."

"Come on, you can show us on the map."

Raider put a hand on CeeCee's shoulder, propelling him toward the street. The mine office was ablaze with lights; the boys had moved operations from Junius' house, which saved some precious time. The brothers stared in astonishment as their father came into the office, striding forcefully. Now that there was something for him to do, he had shed the mantle of senility.

"Junius, where's the map for section four?"

Raider thought of the maps he had left down in the mine, but Junius answered his father's question: "Why, in the safe, Pa." And he came up a moment later with another sheaf of rolled maps, these with yellowed edges.

CeeCee quickly found the map he wanted and unrolled it on Junius' desk as his son made room for him. Raider and Doc read over his shoulders, CeeCee taking the chair as though he had never surrendered possession.

"Right here," he said, tapping the map with a pencil. "You can slip in here, cut across lateral seven, and you'll come out right beyond the main shaft."

"I don't understand," said Junius. "What is this all about? If you want to go down to the main shaft, why don't you use the elevator?"

"I found out Helena has dynamite cached in the mine," said Doc, lying smoothly. No point in revealing their dereliction of duty in not telling about the dynamite before. "We figure from what Bartlett and Helena said that they're going to blow the working tunnels."

"Christ!" said Junius, glancing down at his feet. "If they do, they'll blow the town right off the map!"

"That's the idea," said Raider. "Come on, Doc."

"Wait." Jonathan stood, haggard and showing a tremor in his hands. "I'm coming with you. Jasper, give me a gun."

"Sorry," said Raider. "You'll just be in the way."

"I'm coming," said Jonathan.

"For Christ's sake, stay out of this!" said Junius irritably. "You're no hero. You want to get yourself killed?"

"That's enough!" said CeeCee sharply. "If Jonathan

wants to help out, let him, Junius. He has a share in this mine, too, dammit!"

Junius surrendered, overcome by events and the startling change in his father. Raider saw to it that the three of them were armed with Winchesters from the guard detail and supplied with miner's lamps. He also asked for volunteers, but he wasn't surprised when no one stepped forward. Sawyer brought a buckboard from the mine stable, CeeCee clambering aboard the back. The old man stood during the ride, hanging on to the back of the seat. Shamed by their father's presence, Junius and Jasper also came along.

The opera house proved to be one of the abandoned structures in the lower streets of the town. An overgrown path wound down the side of the mountain below, and CeeCee scampered down it with the agility of a mountain goat.

"Jesus!" said Raider, watching him as he caught at a bush to slow his own slide. "Look at him go!"

"Quite a man," said Doc.

Number four was almost overgrown with brush. The slope below was covered with broken rock where the debris from cutting the shaft had been dumped.

"Thought about buildin' another crusher right here," said CeeCee. "Vein was rich, but it petered out."

They were above the same canyon where the other shaft opened from the cave, but at least half a mile farther down and a hundred yards or more above the canyon floor. No one could come up that slope without the help of ropes.

Their lamps lit, Raider took the lead. The shaft was musty with unused air as they moved inside, and there was nothing to indicate that anyone had been here in the fifteen years since this section of the mine had been abandoned.

A thousand yards in, they reached the lateral shaft and made the turn. To Raider, it seemed like ten thousand. He had not lost any of his fear of enclosed spaces, but he couldn't let it show in front of Doc and Jonathan. He had taken the lead to force himself to face what he feared.

Twenty minutes later, they reached the main shaft and started to trace the tunnels that led to the cave. Just as they reached the place where the lumber had been used to hide the side shaft, Raider signaled for the others to stop. He listened for a minute and then snuffed his light. When they followed suit, they were left in impenetrable darkness.

"Someone's comin'," he whispered. "At least two. Be ready to take them when they come out."

They heard cursing and grunting for nearly a minute before the first light glowed, no brighter than a firefly. Blinking rapidly until his eyes adjusted, Raider let that one come out and turn toward Doc's hiding place. The man carried a box of dynamite.

He was ready for the second man: Raider used his gun as a club, smashing the butt into the back of his head. The man tripped and went flying, smashing the case, while his hat sailed off in a different direction.

The leader spun, and Doc dropped him neatly by slamming the butt plate of his Winchester against his temple. The lamps went out as they hit the ground. Then Jonathan struck a match with a hand that shook worse than before. He managed to relight his lamp while Raider and Doc did the same, and Raider turned the outlaws onto their backs.

"Jack and Mulligan," he said, removing their guns. He threw them as far into the shaft as he could. "Let's go. There may be more comin'."

Raider again led the way, stooping and half-crawling in the more restricted spots. He heard both Doc and Jonathan curse vehemently as they banged heads or elbows or hips on projections. Twice Jonathan lost his light; but each time he managed to get it burning again and came after them.

They had reached Zach's vein when they heard

voices again: three of them this time. There was no place to hide. Killing their lamps, they spread out along the wall nearest the bend in the tunnel and waited. All three of the outlaws carried dynamite; ten seconds later, all three were stretched out on the floor. One groaned, and Doc tapped him again with his rifle until he was still.

Hinckley was one, wearing a new knot to join the one Raider had given him the night before. He didn't know the names of the others, although they had been among those in the kitchen of Brannigan's ranch.

Raider stopped to count. There had been fourteen in the gang, but it wasn't likely that Brannigan and the idiot boy had come along. He had killed Mabbottson the night before and had just put five more out of commission. The gang must have camped in the canyon just outside of town, waiting for Bartlett to bring them their marching orders.

Bartlett had Zelzah; it wasn't likely that he and Helena had stayed around to see the fun. They were undoubtedly on their way to Brannigan's right now, to retrieve as much of the stolen silver as could be moved quickly.

"I figger there's at most five waitin' fer us," he said. He gave his reasoning, and Doc agreed.

"We should have wired the marshal at Carson City to send out a posse."

"That's water under the bridge," said Raider. "It isn't far to the cave. We go slow an' quiet from here on."

They followed him, creeping with guns ready for action. Just short of the last bend, Raider killed his lamp for the last time. Around the corner, he saw daylight ahead. But as the cave grew ahead of them, there was no sign of the other outlaws.

"Maybe the rest went with Bartlett," Raider whispered. "Or maybe they're playin' possum."

Stepping easily to avoid making a noise, he stood

as the cave roof rose over his head and edged toward the side chamber where the dynamite had been stored. But it was empty, the tarpaulin pulled off the cache.

"It don't make sense, Doc," he complained. "I'm gonna poke my nose outside."

The bushes covering the mouth had been trampled flat, the outlaws no longer caring whether it was discovered by someone else. Wondering how they had found the cave, Raider had a sneaking suspicion that CeeCee had spilled a lot more to Helena than he was willing to confess.

He blinked against the bright morning sunlight and started to push his head outside—

A rifle cracked, the slug singing as it ricocheted off the top of the cave entrance and began to slam around inside. Raider heard Doc curse as he drew hastily back inside, and he turned to see Jonathan staring slack-jawed, his face ghastly in color.

"Either of you get hit?" he asked.

"No," said Doc, dusting off his derby. He poked a finger through a hole in the crown. "But any damn closer and you'd be looking for a new partner."

Raider dropped to his belly and elbowed his way back into the mouth of the cave, squinting against the daylight. There was just enough brush left to screen him if he stayed a yard inside. Then he spotted a glint as one of the outlaws perched on the opposite wall of the canyon shifted his rifle. Raider drew up his Winchester, levered a cartridge into the chamber, and took careful aim at the place where the man had to be. After another minute, the outlaw moved again, sticking his head up to look down at one of his fellows.

It was his last mistake. Raider squeezed off a shot, and the slug slammed the man back against the rocks. Perhaps ten seconds later, his rifle came sliding down into the canyon.

"Six down," said Raider.

For several minutes, nothing happened. Then an out-law shouted toward the cave: "You in the mine! Pink!"

"We're listenin'!" answered Raider.

"Throw down your rifles!" He recognized Colby's voice. "We got men behind you—yer cut off!"

"Sorry!" said Raider. "We took care of your men! There ain't nobody left but you and us! I figger four of you, Colby! I'd say the odds are pretty even!"

Colby cursed and began to fire at the cave as fast as he could work the lever. Most of his shots went wild, only two or three finding their way inside. Raider looked back, but Doc and Jonathan had dug them-selves in. They were close enough to add to his fire-power but out of the way of ricochets.

Just when Raider was beginning to think Colby was the only man left in the canyon, he realized another rifle was firing at the cave. Colby switched to his hand-gun, to even worse effect. Not one of his shots came close to the target. The outlaw was well concealed, but Raider waited until he had emptied the pistol, and then he took careful aim at where he ought to be.

The shot went wild. In the ensuing stillness, he heard the click-click as Colby rotated the cylinder of his gun, reloading. He wondered why the man didn't use the rifle, but he hoped there had been a misfire. He counted six shots, and suddenly he came to his feet, breaking out of the cave as the other two outlaws opened up from the floor of the canyon.

They had been waiting for him, suckering him out. And now Colby laughed as Raider desperately half-scrambled, half-rolled down the path that led to the floor of the canyon.

"I told you you was dead, Pink!"

The rifle spoke once, shattering rock less than an inch from Raider's ear. He felt a stinging across his cheek as he dove for cover, rolling again to come to his feet—

—facing a leveled Winchester. One of the other two

outlaws had him trapped. The man grinned as with stunning clarity Raider saw his knuckle whiten to bring tension to the trigger. He drew in what he thought was going to be his last breath—

A small cannon boomed from down the canyon. The outlaw finished pulling the trigger, but the slug went straight into the sky as the heavy-caliber bullet from Zach Gilchrist's Henry blew a hole through his spine. An instant later a Colt Peacemaker spoke from the same direction, pinning down the last of the outlaws in the canyon while Colby leaped to his feet, screaming in outrage.

Aware of the danger, Raider spun on Colby again, firing up. But he was firing into the sun, and the slug missed by a yard. Colby raised the Winchester to his shoulder, sighting straight down at a target he could not miss. There was no place for Raider to go, no cover at all—

But in his eagerness to kill Raider, Colby had forgotten Doc. A single shot rang out from the cave, slamming Colby back against the rocks. He stood there in shock, tears rolling down his cheeks.

"You Pinkerton bastards!" he cried. And then he choked, blood spilling from his mouth. ". . . Pinkerton bastards . . ."

Colby pushed himself away from the wall of the canyon. He tried to bring the rifle to his shoulder, and then he leaned forward and fell, turning end over end until he smashed against the rocks. . . .

CHAPTER TWENTY-NINE

"It's finished, then," said Junius.

While Raider and Doc had been in the shoot-out with the last of Bartlett's gang, Junius had had the presence of mind to wire the marshal in Carson City. Bartlett and Helena had worked feverishly to load as much of the silver as they could into a sturdier wagon than the rig, helped by the girls. Brannigan had stood by, watching the ingots come out of the root cellar.

"Brannigan thought he'd be able to keep what they couldn't carry away," said Doc, smiling.

"How did the woman rope him into her scheme?" asked Jonathan. "He didn't seem the type for a brainy woman like Helena."

"She knew him during the war," said Doc. "Back East. When she learned Brannigan had taken up ranching near here, she sent Bartlett to browbeat him into joining the scheme."

They sat in the mine office, Raider and Doc, the three Coffin brothers, and CeeCee. The old man was in the center spot, beaming with pride over his role in wiping out the outlaw gang.

"You'd think the old bastard led the shoot-out," Raider had said this morning. For the last two days, CeeCee had once again been cock of the walk.

Now CeeCee said, "I still say those she-whelps was in on it from the beginnin'. Dammit, they oughta be behind bars with Helena, before they skin some man outa his hide an' wallet an' his eyeteeth."

Zelzah and Moravia had been set free at Raider's insistence. "There's no proof they were involved," he said, for the twentieth time. "And Moravia did save my life."

CeeCee snorted. "Pulled the wool over your eyes, you mean!"

The crushers rumbled outside the office, rattling the walls of the surrounding buildings. The silver had all been there except those few bars salvaged by Zach and a few more the gang had missed in the other robberies. It had been moved to the vaults of the Carson City mint, its original destination. Recovery had come in time for the Queen to meet all outstanding contracts.

Zach and Amity had shown up in the nick of time, despite Zuch's protestations to Raider when he had deposited Hermione that he intended to stay far away from the Queen and the Coffins. Amity later confessed that it was either come or see Hermione come without them. Neither could take that.

Helena, Billy Bartlett, and Brannigan were in the Carson City jail. The outlaws who had survived the shoot-out were under lock and key in Seth Morgan's cells, complaining bitterly about the stench and the food. Leaving the boardinghouse that morning, Raider had heard someone say, almost in awe, that Seth had finally been shamed into taking a bath.

The gang members who hadn't been so lucky were laid out in the back room of the barber shop. Now that Doc had finished taking their photographs for the case record, they could be buried. He would get pictures of the three in the Carson City jail when he passed through the town.

That left only the final judgment of the trial to close out the case record. Another case solved. Wagner would be happy.

"They'll hang," said Jasper with satisfaction. "The lot of them, and good riddance."

CeeCee shook his head. "Not Helena. She'll work her wiles on th' judge an' th' jury. They'll never hang her, not twelve men. That woman was put on this earth by Satan hisself just to devil men. She's got too much of his work to finish."

There was a moment of silence; then Jasper got up and offered to refill glasses. Doc and Raider declined, but the others were in a mood to celebrate.

"I have to say," said Junius, "I didn't think much of the job you two were doing. But it came out all right in the end. Yessir, it came out all right."

"I hope you'll think the same when you get the bill," said Doc.

"We will," said Junius. "And we'll pay it, no matter how much it comes to, and gladly."

Doc stood. "Well, gentlemen, it's time Raider and I moved on. I won't say it's been a pleasure, because there were some damn skinny minutes there when I thought we wouldn't solve the case. But we did; and now it's time to say good-bye."

He offered his hand to CeeCee and then to the others; Raider did the same. Then, with a final chorus of good-byes from the four Coffins, the partners walked out of the Coffin Queen's office for the last time, to breathe deeply and appreciatively of the June air.

"I'd say it was coolin' a bit," said Raider.

"Yes," said Doc. "It'll make traveling easier. What say we stop in the Silver Bucket for a drink, partner, before we hit the trail?"

"You go on ahead, Doc. I'll catch up to you in Carson City, and we'll have that drink there. Right now I got . . . uh . . . somebody else to say good-bye to."

The black horse was tied to the hitching rail outside the office; the Studebaker waited in the yard, Judith in the traces. The mule pricked up her ears as Doc approached, whickering. He paused to scratch behind each ear as he watched Raider ride out, and then he fed Judith a carrot from his pocket.

"Time to move on, old girl," he said.

Judith whickered again as Doc climbed to the seat and took up the reins. Wagner hadn't had a chance to reply to the semifinal report Doc had forwarded by wire yesterday. Doc did not want to be around when the parsimonious manager of the Chicago office got his expense account for three weeks in Virginia City. This time Wagner might well forget to congratulate them on a tough job well done.

He snapped the reins, and Judith leaned into the traces. Coffin Canyon had come to life again; the miners were underground, where they belonged, and prosperity had returned to a town that had almost been killed by outlaws. Bartlett and the others really should have silver tombstones erected over their graves, for greed for silver had done them in.

Doc whistled a tuneless song as Judith pulled the brightly painted apothecary wagon out of town and started down the steep grade. The fork came up that would let them take the main road, the shortest way down to Carson City, or the longer way, past Graveyard Gap. A mile or more below, where the road snaked around the bulk of the mountain, he spotted a black-clad rider pushing a black horse for all it was worth. Smiling, Doc took the Gap road.

And several hours later he smiled again as he spotted smoke spiraling out of the canyon below Graveyard Gap, coming from Zach Gilchrist's cabin. Doc was well aware that Raider had tossed both Zelzah and Moravia, and he would have bet most of a month's pay that right now he was bedded down between Amity and Hermione.

He thought of Helena, and his smile grew wistful. She wouldn't hang, but by the time she got out of jail, her beauty would be gone. Doc sighed.

"Helena was some woman, Judith. I'll take quality over quantity every time. Right, girl?"

Judith hee-hawed her agreement.

J.D. HARDIN

"THE MOST EXCITING WESTERN WRITER SINCE LOUIS L'AMOUR"
—JAKE LOGAN

☑	16840 BLOOD, SWEAT AND GOLD	$1.95
✓	16842 BLOODY SANDS	$1.95
—	16882 BULLETS, BUZZARDS, BOXES OF PINE	$1.95
—	16843 FACE DOWN IN A COFFIN	$1.95
✓	16844 THE GOOD, THE BAD, AND THE DEADLY	$1.95
—	16799 HARD CHAINS, SOFT WOMEN	$1.95
✓	16881 THE MAN WHO BIT SNAKES	$1.95
—	16861 RAIDER'S GOLD	$1.95
—	16883 RAIDER'S HELL	$1.95
—	16767 RAIDER'S REVENGE	$1.95
✓	16555 THE SLICK AND THE DEAD	$1.50
—	16869 THE SPIRIT AND THE FLESH	$1.95

 PLAYBOY PAPERBACKS
Book Mailing Service
P.O. Box 690 Rockville Centre, New York 11571

NAME _Mark D Licker_

ADDRESS _179-45 Hillside ave_

CITY _Jamaica_ STATE _New York_ ZIP_

Please enclose 50¢ for postage and handling if one book is ordered; 25¢ for each additional book. $1.50 maximum postage and handling charge. No cash, CODs or stamps. Send check or money order.

Total amount enclosed: $ _8.70_